GUNS ON THE GUADALUPE

ALSO BY MARK GREATHOUSE

GUNS ON THE GUADALUPE

JUSTICE ON THE RIVER

THE TUMBLEWEED SAGAS
BOOK 9

MARK GREATHOUSE

WOLFPACK
PUBLISHING
— EST 2013 —

Guns on the Guadalupe: Justice on the River
Paperback Edition
Copyright © 2025 by Mark Greathouse

Wolfpack Publishing
1707 E. Diana Street
Tampa, Florida 33610

www.wolfpackpublishing.com

Paperback ISBN 979-8-89567-220-4
Ebook ISBN 979-8-89567-219-8
LCCN 9798895672204

Dedicated with love to my wife, Carolyn, and to our two sons, Mike and Matt.

MAP OF TEXAS

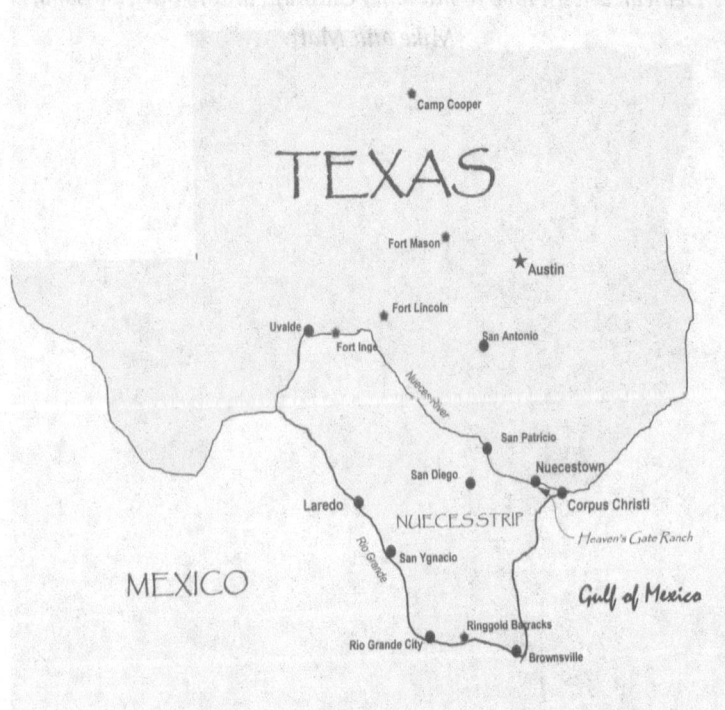

The vast Nueces Strip serves as the primary setting for the Tumbleweed Sagas. The Strip was also called Wild Horse Desert, owing to the millions of Mustangs that roamed its prairies. *(Sketch by Mark Greathouse)*

NUECESTOWN

Nuecestown, Texas, established in 1852 by English and German settlers, was developed by Corpus Christi founder Colonel Henry Kinney along the Nueces River as a ferry crossing. Mostly thanks to the railroad passing it by, it's now a "ghost town" marked only by historical markers. All that remains is a preserved schoolhouse and the old Nuecestown Cemetery. By 1898, the town was struggling economically *(Sketch by Mark Greathouse)*

THE CAST

Lucas Dunn Jr.—*Goes by the nickname "Junior." The proverbial fruit doesn't grow far from the tree, as Junior follows in the lawman footsteps of his legendary Texas Ranger father.*

Cassie McCully Dunn—*Daughter of Grant McCully, who owns a ranch near Heaven's Gate. Cassie is married to Junior. Family ties complicate our story.*

Grant McCully—*Cassie's father. McCully is a successful rancher.*

Lucas Long Luke Dunn—*Was one of the greatest Texas Ranger Captains ever, having gained repute as Indian fighter and respected lawman. Comanche called him Ghost-Who-Rides. Luke builds Heaven's Gate Ranch and has eleven children with his wife Elisa.*

Elisa Corrigan Dunn—*Married Luke Dunn after losing her family to frontier rigors, including fighting off Comanche and hired killers.*

Joseph Kilkenny—*Notorious land schemer and erstwhile killer and rustler.*

Diana Kilkenny—*Beautiful but devious temptress.*

Garth Jones—*A gunfighter for hire.*

Sam Chambliss—*Local rancher concerned over land grabbing. Owns Running Circle Ranch alongside the Guadalupe River.*

Amy Chambliss—*Sam Chambliss's wife.*

Cord Chambliss—*The Chambliss's ne'er-do-well lawyer son.*

HISTORICAL CHARACTERS

Bass Reeves—*Famed Black US Deputy Marshal who forged a legendary career capturing desperadoes, mostly in Oklahoma. Notably, he could not read, but would memorize the writs he served.*

Charles Culberson—*Followed Jim Hogg and then Joseph Clay Stiles Blackburn as governor of Texas. He ran afoul of the Democratic Party over his opposition to the Ku Klux Klan.*

John Reynolds Hughes—*Became the longest-serving Texas Ranger captain. Hughes dealt with Comanche and Apache over his years as rancher and lawman. He was a sergeant in the Frontier Battalion down along the Texas/Mexico border until 1893, when he was promoted to captain.*

Emilio Forto—*Sheriff of Cameron County, TX and later mayor of Brownsville.*

Archer Parr—*Known as "Archie," he established a political dynasty in what* *became Jim Wells County and led to decades of Democratic Party control through means fair and foul.*

Stephen Powers—*Political power broker exercising tight control over goings-on in Corpus Christi. He had close ties with Archie Parr and Jim Wells.*

John William Vann—*Tax Collector and Sheriff of Kerr County, TX, from 1892 through 1902.*

Judge Isaac Parker—*Known as the "hanging judge," Parker delivered law and order out of Fort Smith, Arkansas. Bass Reeves reported to him.*

John McTiernan—*Sheriff of Nueces County, TX, from 1896 to 1902.*

Henry Thomas—*Sheriff of Galveston, Texas.*

THEME

Justice:
_The quality of being just, impartial, or fair per the principle or
ideal of just dealing or proper action in conformance to a principle
or ideal as defined by the law or to truth, fact, or reason._

YOU'RE INVITED

Howdy,

It's been a pleasure to share the first seven Tumbleweed Sagas featuring the exploits of my namesake legendary father, Texas Ranger Lucas Dunn. From here on, I reckon to share my own experiences wearing the Texas Ranger badge. You can call me Junior. In fact, this can be called Tumbleweed Sagas: Junior's Story.

Guns on the Guadalupe: Justice on the River picks up my story from *Lonestar Vigilante: Justice Texas Style*. It offers a twisted tale of intrigue, as I must solve the mystery of a series of connected killings. The Nueces Strip encompassing the southern tip of Texas by this time could be said to be afire economically, as agriculture, railroads, communications, and black gold spawned ever greater growth. Communications? While the telegraph expanded its reach, it was the soon-to-be-ubiquitous telephone that was beginning to make its presence felt mostly in the larger Texas cities. And black gold? The *Lucas Gusher* at Spindletop Hill in 1901 near Beaumont would usher in the Texas oil era.

Gushers of oil became ever more common, creating gushers of money in bank accounts.

Barbed wire had made its appearance on the Nueces Strip fifteen years earlier and was creating a topographical patchwork of pasture and farm. The resulting range wars, fence cuttings, and water rights battles fostered lawbreaking challenges that tested the mettle of many a lawman. Lynching and worse bore evidence to a rise in vigilante justice, as frustrated and fearful citizens took the law into their own hands.

It's 1896, and the Nueces Strip could be inhospitable six-ways to Sunday. The similarities between natural and human dangers were often striking. Imagine the intense eyes and writhing coils of a rattlesnake on the hunt. A rabbit looks about innocently, unaware. The snake's forked tongue picks up vibrations in the air. Patience...of sorts. The moment of attack must be exactly right. Only an infinitesimal twitch of the tip of his rattle-bedecked tail reveals the tension in the beast. He dares not indulge a blink of eyes. A sudden uncoiling, mouth open, fangs exposed, and the rattlesnake is fed. In its vast silence, the Nueces Strip sucks it all in. And the Guadalupe River defines the far northern reaches of this zone of lawlessness and mayhem.

Application of the law could too often be horrifically fast or mind-bogglingly slow. The accused lawbreaker could as easily meet his end at an impromptu necktie party as be convicted in a court of law. Fingerprint matching and DNA databases were nonexistent. My own cousin, Red John Dunn, capped off a ten-year enlistment with the Texas Rangers under Captain Bland Chamberlain and later Captain Leander McNelly with several instances of involvement with vigilante justice. Taking the law into one's own hands was expeditious but illegal and fraught with far too many instances of innocent men being on the wrong end of a rope or bullet. Dunn himself was tried twice for murder and acquitted both times.

In *Guns on the Guadalupe: Justice on the River*, I'm right pleased to share my story of following in my legendary father's lawman footsteps and seeking to make significant headway in bringing justice to the Nueces Strip. Blood, as shed by both innocent and evil men, colors the Strip. Desperate killers, rustlers, disease, and savages are part and parcel to my life. Just about anywhere I ride, death could be reaching for my reins. While it could be said that I emulate my father in building considerable notoriety and creating enemies by virtue of my success in bringing lawbreakers to justice, I am very much my own man and have established reliable allies.

While the *Cast of Historical Characters* provides some helpful true-to-life framework to the life and times on the Nueces Strip, woven into *Guns on the Guadalupe: Justice on the River* are actual settlers of the frontier as drawn from my own extensive Texas family ancestry. Such real-life characters coupled with actual events have served to reinforce the fictional setting with a strong dose of reality.

For anyone of a mind that the frontier had been won, they had a second think coming. The wild prairies and hills of Texas were alive and kicking, lawbreaking was very much in abundance, and what one might call the residuals of old wild west justice prevailed. It's in this setting that vigilante justice remained strong, for better or worse.

Kindly,
	Lucas Dunn Jr.

GUNS ON THE GUADALUPE

PROLOGUE

I TOOK my time rubbing down and talking to Tornado before returning to the big house. I found myself swelling with pride just a bit, as I thought back on the past few months. I'd solved a mystery that had baffled the best lawmen around these parts by bringing to justice a cunning vigilante. Skill? Some. Luck? Some of that, too. My father, a legendary Texas Ranger, was quite justly bust-a-button proud.

Cassie greeted me at the door with baby Sean in her arms. "Did you see Captain Hughes?" She laid their newborn son in a cradle by the kitchen table.

"Yep," I responded with a nod and a smile.

"And?"

"I gave him our answer." I led her over to the chest against the wall that framed what served as an entry foyer. Despite the wood having expanded thanks to the South Texas humidity, I managed to ceremoniously pull open the top drawer. I drew the polished silver Texas Ranger badge from my pocket, put it to my mouth and huffed upon it, buffed it on my shirt, and gently placed it in the drawer.

With that, Cassie wrapped her arms tightly around me.

Feeling her against me, combined with the adrenaline rush of having made a final decision on our future, caused me serious arousal.

"Not just yet, cowboy." Cassie smiled provocatively. *Men*, she thought. Two days after childbirth, and her man was roused to passion. It held plenty of appeal but would have to wait.

I looked down into her crystal blue eyes and figured what she was thinking. I kissed her long and hard. "They shouldn't make new mothers so danged sexy," I whispered.

"Let's fill your other appetite, Lucas Dunn. Dinner's just about ready." She pulled away, patted my butt, and pushed me toward the dining table.

Captain John Hughes sat tall in the saddle, as he led his men by a column of twos south from Corpus Christi. They were headed back to the Rio Grande to deal with some threatening stirrings by a troublemaker named Pancho Villa.

His lieutenant pulled alongside. "If I may, Captain?"

"What's on your mind, Bert?"

"Will Lucas Dunn be joining us?"

Hughes cracked a broad grin. "Junior? One of these days, Bert. One of these days." He looked off into the distant horizon. "Texas Rangers never give up the badge." He gave an extra nudge to his horse and pulled ahead of the lieutenant. "Never give up the badge," he said softly to himself.

ONE
MURDER MOST FOUL

DARKNESS SHROUDED the banks of the Guadalupe River as it meandered its way through the very heart of Texas. The air hung heavy with mid-spring dampness, and the moonlight turned most anything standing above ground into a silhouette. The canoe laid up on the northern bank of the shallow-flowing river was pretty much an antique for these parts. It was constructed of birch bark over an ash frame sealed with spruce gum. Someone with more obsession for tradition than sense had likely carted the contraption from back east. The birch-bark canoe had been invented many moons ago by the Anishinaabe tribe of the eastern Algonquian people. The eastern tribes especially had preferred the birch-bark canoe to the dugouts of the Mohawks and Mohicans because they were lighter for ease of portaging, flexible enough to absorb heavier seas in open waters, and had a shallower draft, enabling them to glide smoothly over peaceful waters. Hidden in the reeds beside the craft hunched a shadowy figure. He held his pocket watch up to catch the moonlight. Nine o'clock! Where the Sam-hell were they?

The Guadalupe cuts a deep swath through what folks referred to as the Hill Country. It meandered more than 400 miles from the Edwards Aquifer to San Antonio Bay and Gulf of Mexico. Might say it offered an ideal waterway for a birch-bark canoe. Up near the headwaters of the river, high bluffs overlooked its path.

Just northwest of Kerrville, a well-attired man stood at the top of one of those bluffs. He puffed on a cigar and cast an impatient eye on the gathering clouds. He oozed money and wealth. His silver spurs caught the moonlight. Otherwise, he was nearly indistinguishable from the silhouettes of brush and trees around him. He pulled back his coat and drew an engraved gold watch from a pocket in his black brocaded vest, checked the time, and glanced about expectantly. Where was he? A light rain began to fall. Just a drop or two here and there, then a tad more. There was no sound but the rain talking to the leaves. The night seemed to have become darker. Surrounding rocks blackened with the wetness.

A single gunshot bruised the night air. The well-dressed man on the bluff clutched his chest and looked down in the dim light at the dark stain already beginning to spread on his fancy silk vest. His eyes widened. He realized that he'd just been killed. He sank ever-so-slowly to his knees, as though fearful of soiling his neatly pressed pin-striped trousers. Breathing became ever-quicker and more difficult. He was determined not to fall from the bluff. He extinguished his cigar, allowed himself to slowly meet the earth beneath him, and blacked out.

Two shadows emerged. They grabbed the man under the arms and dragged him down from the bluff to the waiting canoe.

"About time, dammit," growled the man guarding the canoe.

"Just shut up and do your job, Fr..." said one man, nearly blurting out the name of the man at the canoe.

"What did you do with your rifle?"

"Pitched it way out in the middle of the river. No dog gonna find it," said the shooter through a toothless grin.

"Any witnesses?"

"Not so we could tell none," said the toothless killer.

"Put him in the canoe."

The two men dutifully hauled the body into the canoe.

"Can I have his boots? They sure be fancy," said the shooter, looking down at his own muddied leathers.

"Just leave the body be. You've done your job."

"Guess we'll be on our way. Sure could use a drink."

"Sounds well-deserved," offered the man as he prepared to launch the body-laden canoe. Suddenly, he stood tall. "Permit me to contribute," he said with an evil smile. With that, he made a motion to his pocket. The Derringer filled his palm. He couldn't miss at this range. The shots echoed off the bluffs, and two bodies thudded to the ground. The sound of the gunshots likely didn't really matter. In but seconds, he'd pushed off and headed downriver to deposit the body far from prying eyes. As to the two dead accomplices—they were of no concern. Somebody would eventually find the bodies.

He looked at his own pocket watch. Ten minutes after nine o'clock. He was on schedule.

TWO
FLOATERS

OLD SOL THREW his line into the river, and sat back to enjoy the soothing effect of the sun glinting from the ripples. Leaves and branches occasionally floated by. He figured to catch three or four bass in short order. Fish and eggs for breakfast suited his palate just fine. Dumb fish simply couldn't resist his bait. The formula was a closely guarded family secret.

Something a tad different caught his eye. What was that thing gliding downstream but a couple of yards from the shoreline? He pulled in his line, shed his boots, and waded in.

"Holy Mother of God!" he exclaimed upon close inspection. He reflexively drew back.

Two bloated, deathly pale faces stared back at him from the water. Around them was some sort of wood and bark contraption that might have been some sort of boat.

Sol vomited.

Gathering his wits best he could, he guided what was left of the boat toward shore. No way was he going to touch the bodies inside. As he pulled the contraption ashore, he found himself further repelled by the odor of death. The boat appeared to actually be a canoe—its bottom ripped enough to have mostly sunk it.

The old man held his nose and scanned the two bodies. A beautiful gold watch hung by a chain from the pocket of one victim. Sol glanced about. No one was around. He carefully disengaged the pocket watch from its deceased owner. It was wet, but likely could be dried out. He'd always wanted a fine timepiece. Sol stuffed the watch in his pocket, grabbed his boots and fishing rod, and headed up toward the shoreline road.

Sheriff John Vann scratched his bearded chin thoughtfully, as he studied the bodies laid out before him. It wasn't every day that floaters littered the Guadalupe River. And what were they doing in a birch-bark canoe? Both victims had been shot. But by whom and when and where? The corpses were in decent shape despite being water-logged. By his studied consideration, he guessed they'd fallen victim at some time during the night. The bullet wounds suggested two different weapons. Vann's hand went to the brim of his hat, which he doffed to wipe a bead of sweat from his brow with his forearm.

Vann had been sheriff for nearly four years, but this was unlike any crime he'd had to deal with. He wasn't one to jump to conclusions, but the use of two different weapons suggested two killers or perhaps even a double-cross by a single killer. Both victims were unarmed, though the man with the vest had a stretched pocket, suggesting he might have had a weapon. He noticed a bit of grass and river mud stuck to the boot heels of one victim. Also, there was a tear in a buttonhole where a watch fob might have been attached. He tried not to breathe the foul odors, as he dug through the victim's pockets. Nothing.

"Yo! John!" a voice called from higher up on the shoreline. "Got a report of two bodies about a mile upstream."

Vann had a reputation as a dependable lawman but never let his ego get in the way of good sense. Four bodies in one morning? He began to think that a call to Texas Ranger Captain John Hughes just might be in order. He'd heard that Hughes had some young-buck Ranger that solved some vigilante case. Lord knows, this situation was shaping up to be beyond the sleuthing capabilities of the Kerr County Sheriff's Office.

"Bag'em, Slim," he called out to one of the coroner's men. Vann would head upstream to check out the other two bodies. He'd tethered his horse at the top of the path. The rains had stopped, but distant clouds threatened more. Given the capricious weather, he nevertheless decided that walking would give him time to think. His horse didn't even need the reins held, he just dutifully walked behind the sheriff. Vann's practiced eyes took in the town as he ambled along the street. Was there something unusual going on?

Kerrville had sure changed over the past half-century. The early settlers had made shingles from the plentiful cypress lining the river. The area was judged by many to be the prettiest part of the Hill Country. In addition to the looming ghostlike cypress, lining the banks were plentiful stands of sycamore, pecan, elm, basswood, walnut, and more. Oak and juniper with grasslands could be found on higher elevations. The trees offered a generous nesting habitat for birds. Vann fully appreciated this place he had called home for many years. It sure offered some fine hunting, including white-tailed deer mixed in with varmints like coyote, gray fox, skunk, raccoon, opossum, bobcat, and armadillo.

Vann appreciated how the early pioneers had first built the town near a bluff just north of and overlooking the river. The folks eventually named the town Kerrville in honor of James Kerr, a major in the Texas Revolution. It wasn't long before a fellow named Charles Schreiner established a family-operated empire that included freighting enterprises, retail and wholesale goods, banking, ranching, marketing, and even brokering operations. The War Between the States had slowed development for a brief time, but Kerrville was quick to recover, as demand built for lumber and produce. Fewer Indian raids and expansion of cattle and sheep ranching fueled its rise. Vann smiled, as he recalled Kerrville at one time being called the Mohair Capital, as it shipped out huge quantities of mohair via the newly arrived San Antonio and Aransas Pass Railway. Shucks, they'd even begun to receive city water a couple of years back, and they'd just started a telephone service. Kerrville was becoming quite modern, but Vann realized that law enforcement wasn't keeping up.

He arrived at the top of the path leading back down to the river, where a deputy was watching over the two bodies and keeping spectators at bay. He left his horse ground-hitched and made his way down to the water's edge. "Mornin' Dave. Whatcha got here?"

"Small bore, Sheriff Vann. I figure it was likely one of them pocket pistols."

That fit with Vann's observation of the vest on one of the victims downriver. By his count, as many as three firearms were involved. He scratched his beard. Who shot who, lingered in his head?

"There's more, Sheriff. There are drag tracks in the brush leading up to yonder bluff," he said with a finger pointing toward the landmark. "I followed them up, and there's some blood on the rocks where someone had done quite a bit of bleeding."

Vann absorbed the deputy's information. Dragging a man through the brush could account for the mud and grass stuck in one of the downriver victim's boot heels. "Any witnesses?" Vann knew it was a perfunctory question. He had to ask it.

"Nope."

"How about ID?"

"Clean, Sheriff."

"Anyone around here know these men?" asked Vann, as he scanned the half dozen bystanders.

"The one over there looks like Sam Waltz, but I can't be sure."

Identification was understandably difficult, given the slight bloating that had already occurred. "Let's get'em to the coroner for cleaning up, have pictures taken of all four men, and see if anyone in town knows them." Vann looked up the hill and noted the coroner's black wagon arriving as though on cue.

"What do you think, Red?" Vann asked the coroner. He hated this place. The coroner's laboratory was dark and dingy and smelled of formaldehyde. Red Schultz was a nice enough guy, but his vocation held no appeal for Vann.

"Going take some time, John. You probably already figured that we're dealing with three guns. It'll take some digging to figure the sequence. Then, we can get to who shot who and when." Schultz tried to look reassuring. "I can say that none of them shot themselves. No powder burns."

Vann nodded. Schultz's judgment meant that there was a killer loose in Kerr County. Worse, was the uncertainty of whether the killer could be hanging around or have high-tailed it. The latter action made the best sense. The perpetrator could already be outside the sheriff's jurisdiction. This crime was big. Vann reluctantly admitted to himself that assistance was necessary. Last he'd heard, Captain John Hughes was leading his Texas Rangers to Brownsville. Vann reckoned to use one of those new-fangled things they called a telephone to reach out to Hughes, if the doggone Apache hadn't cut the lines.

THREE
HEADLINE

THE DRAWER HAUNTED ME. It was as though the Texas Ranger badge gave off a penetrating aura that oozed from the drawer's unlit interior. Yes, I'd promised Cassie that I wouldn't pin it on again. Maybe being a lawman was simply in my blood. It sure felt like it. Maybe, it was part of having grown up with my legendary Texas Ranger father.

I took a last sip of coffee, gave Cassie a kiss, patted Sean on his sweet cheek, and ambled off to the barn. There were chores to tend to, and I didn't have time to sit around dreaming of could-have-beens. I swung the door open and led an excited Tornado from his stall to the corral. A sugar cube temporarily satisfied the big stallion's yearning for attention. I returned to the barn, grabbed a shovel, and began mucking stalls. They didn't write about this part of the cowboy life in the dime-store books. I leaned on the shovel handle for a moment, just thinking. Life was good. Why even think of turning it upside down.

Mucking finished, I looked over at my favorite saddle. It sure was in need of a cleaning. The goldarned thing had seen better days. The thorny thickets and dusty soil of

Heaven's Gate Ranch took a toll on man, horse, and saddle. Even my chaps hanging alongside the saddle were long past their prime. I glanced out the big window at the rear end of the barn. I needed to head out and check the beeves on the northernmost range, so I decided to take care of cleaning the saddle later. Besides, I was anxious to climb aboard Tornado and put some distance between myself and that goldarned drawer.

Cassie had packed me some jerky and biscuits to snack on and hold my appetite until dinner. Of course, the hunger in my stomach wasn't the appetite she was most interested in. I admitted to myself that I'd sorely missed her warm body entwined with mine but was making up for lost time. She'd put me off just a bit after Sean's birth, and that whet my hunger for her as mere thoughts of a meal never could.

I soon found himself aboard my big Appaloosa on an easy trot to check on those cattle. "What do you think about that badge, Tornado?" I asked sort of rhetorically.

Tornado gave a bit of a nicker as though understanding my thoughts.

"Yep. I do love ranching, and I did make a promise to Cassie. But, if the opportunity were to come…" I looked off thoughtfully toward the horizon, scratching my chin in a manner similar to my father's habit.

"Lookee there, Tornado!" I exclaimed, as we came upon a cow with a newborn calf. "Ain't that a wonderful sight," I intoned. The cow was busy licking the afterbirth from the wobbly-legged youngster that seemed fully intent on getting his first drink. I found myself ever-amazed at the wonders of procreation. There was a romance to nature. Naturally, it brought my thinking back to figuring a romantic interlude after our evening meal. It was warm enough that I just might lure Cassie back to that deep pool in the stream near the ranch house. I vaguely recalled that my dad lured my mother there early in their courtship. Cassie and I could enjoy a nearly full moon and myriad stars with a touch of wine and just ourselves. For the present, these musings lifted my mind from that omnipresent badge in the dresser drawer.

I decided to herd the cow back to the ranch, as the calf would be especially vulnerable to varmints out in the ruggedness of this part of the ranch. Money was still tight owing to drought, and every bit of livestock was vital to survival. As I thought on this, I noticed three buzzards circling high and a bit ahead of me. I decided the cow and her calf could wait the few minutes it would take to see what interested the birds.

I nudged Tornado forward and found myself instinctively slipping the 1895 Winchester from my saddle scabbard. I let it lie across my lap and against the saddle horn as I moved forward. Tornado stepped carefully around cacti and mesquite, though his ears pricked up, and he began acting uncharacteristically nervous as they drew closer to the place I figured the buzzards were interested in. "Easy boy," I whispered, as I lifted the rifle and chambered a round.

We broke into a clearing with a creek running up its middle. There was a mountain lion chowing down on a deer. There was no sense disturbing the cat's dinnertime, so I backed Tornado away. I could have shot the cat. He was what they called an apex predator. The food chain fell away beneath him. I'd hunted for mountain lion or cougar or puma or whatever folks preferred to call them with my dad and Buffalo Watts, but shooting a peacefully feeding cat just didn't seem sporting. Likely, it was just as well that I was now aware of the big cat being on the ranch, and it firmed my resolve to guide mother and calf back to the safety of the cattle corral alongside the barn.

Cassie didn't bother to knock at the door to her folks' home. After all, it had been her home since she'd been a little tyke playing with horses, goats, and rabbits before succumbing to her mother's demands for a more traditional womanly upbringing. She could cook and sew and churn butter, but still loved the thrill of riding across the prairies with the wind in her hair. And she could shoot the hair off a flea.

"Morning, Mom," she called.

"Why Cassie, dear," she mocked, "don't you ever bother to knock, dear?"

Cassie laughed and poured herself a cup of coffee.

"You're up to something," stated Mother McCully, as she took Sean from her daughter's arms. "My, but he's growing right big," she exclaimed, pretending to be surprised.

"Do you still have that recipe for what the cowboys used to call bear sign?"

Mother McCully's expression turned a tad serious. "You mean donuts?"

Cassie nodded.

"Let me fetch the recipe," she said as she rummaged through the recipe box beside the stove. "What's wrong?"

"What makes you think something's wrong?" responded Cassie.

Her mother flashed one of those *don't try to put anything over on me* expressions.

"I fear Junior might go back to the badge," Cassie admitted.

Her mother looked at the little face nestled in her grandmotherly arms. "Can't imagine Lucas risking it, sweetie." She knew better. Junior had his father's blood running in his veins. If called back to the badge, he couldn't resist. The challenge of bringing lawbreakers to justice was strong.

"I walk by the bedroom chest of drawers." She paused. "I know the badge lies in the top drawer. I can feel it calling to him. I feel it to my core."

Mother McCully shook her head dismayingly. "What will be will be, child. You know he loves you. Is being a Texas Ranger the real Lucas Dunn, Junior. Every man is unique, Cassie. First and foremost is that he loves you and you alone, even more than himself. I saw that the first time you met."

Cassie sighed. Mother McCully was right. "I think I'm pregnant," Cassie confessed.

I stopped at the mailbox by the gate and watched as cow and calf ambled up the lane ahead of me. The mail service had come a long way, as rural carriers delivered directly to ranches within easy rides of town post offices. Roads wended their way around parcels set apart by barbed wire fences. There was nothing of special importance in the box this day, save for a newspaper. I was about to stuff it in my saddlebag but couldn't resist a peek. *MURDERS ON THE GUADALUPE* blared the headline. That was attention-grabbing! "Four found dead!" I whispered incredulously, as though Tornado could understand me. "Looks like Sheriff Vann's calling in the Texas Rangers, Tornado." The big stallion nickered in reply. The headline had seemed to fly from the newspaper.

Dared I share the newspaper with Cassie. I could hardly avoid it, and she'd surely catch my lawman reaction to the Kerrville events. I urged Tornado to a trot, as we headed up the lane to the barn behind the momma longhorn and her little one. The cow found her way into the corral with her newborn calf following directly behind. I dismounted, closed the corral gate, and led the big stallion into his stall. As I curried and fed Tornado, I found my thoughts straying to Kerrville and the apparent mystery that lingered there. What my father would do or, more correctly, would have done? Then again, I'd made a promise to Cassie. I chuckled at the thought and shrugged, as I hadn't even been asked by Captain Hughes. That might never happen. I patted Tornado, stuck the rolled-up newspaper under my arm, and headed to the ranch house.

The delicious aroma of dinner greeted me, as I strode through the front door. "Got a newborn up in the north pasture and brought them to the corral," I stated emphatically. "Mountain lion running around up there." It was as much to announce my entry as to let Cassie know that I'd had a good day. I dropped the newspaper on the small table in the foyer. I didn't notice that it had unrolled to reveal the headline.

"Have a seat, sweetheart. Dinner's nearly ready," she called from the kitchen.

I poured myself a cup of coffee and sat at the table.

Cassie soon appeared with Sean at her breast. She placed a plate heaped with dinner fare before me, then turned to retrieve her own.

"Wait," I said. "Sit." I directed and pushed my plate to her place. I walked to the kitchen and fixed a plate for her, not quite so much food, of course.

Cassie sat, reflecting on her loving husband's thoughtful gesture. She mustered an inviting smile, as I sat opposite her at the small table. "Are you..."

"Up for some wine and a swim? Yes." I finished her sentence and took her free hand in mine. "I love you, Cassie McCully Dunn."

★★

Sean went to sleep quickly. Out here, miles from what folks called civilization, we had no worries about leaving him alone. We wouldn't be going that far, and we would hear any trouble.

The swimming hole was all that we'd remembered. We sat on a blanket, looking up at the stars. I held my wine-glass up to the moon. The red wine shimmered in the moonlight. Cassie did the same, finally clinking her glass against mine. We kissed, first lightly then ever more passionately. My shirt came off first, then her blouse. The wine spilled. No matter. We slid into the cool swirling waters, allowing them to flow gently over our naked bodies. She stood in the waist-deep water with moonlight glistening from her wet shoulders and ample breasts. I motioned to the blanket. First, our naked, wet bodies joined as one in the swirling, warm waters of the swimming hole. Oh, but her flesh against mine was heaven-sent. We made our way to the blanket and released our passions into each other. Fully consumed, we lay back unclothed beneath the starry sky. It was so quiet we could hear the stars twinkling. It was a moment of total peace, of love, of a closeness that only true lovers can know.

Cassie rolled over and lay one leg across my body. Her hand stroked my well-muscled chest. *My God, but he's sexy*, she thought. She kissed my ear, bit it gently, and whispered. "Lucas, we're pregnant."

My eyes opened wide. Thoughts of Texas Rangers became furthest from my mind, as I turned to Cassie and embraced her. My manhood arose to the occasion, and we once again consumed ourselves in passion. We were oblivious to all but our writhing bodies immersed in our own love cadence. She gently broke free, pushed me onto my back, climbed onto my hips, and absorbed my manhood.

We were soon spent. We'd been fully consumed to our passions. Unbeknownst to us, the mountain lion had watched from afar. A rattlesnake had slithered by, and a couple of coyotes had slaked their thirsts at the swimming hole. Ours was love. Some say that love is sex, need, romance, security, and more all joined together. With Cassie, my love for her was all of these things yet none of them separately. I'd watched my mother and my dad. They raised ten children, and there was a true love between them. As I grew, I realized what they had endured in constant wonder, discovery, joy, and the simple peace found in living. Every day was an adventure for them. Even his long days away as a Texas Ranger on the Nueces Strip mattered not in the intensity and fullness of their love. I yearned to share that sort of love with Cassie.

FOUR
RETURN TO THE BADGE

CASSIE LAID the newspaper down as she consumed the final morsels of her breakfast. I had saddled Tornado and ridden out with a couple of ranch hands to tend the herd on the south range. The phone rang. She was apprehensive about how the phone interrupted what she saw as normal life. Normal? It seemed that normal was a fluid concept. It could change in a heartbeat. The phone rang again.

"Hello?" she said, as she picked up the earpiece and bent into the receiver.

"You hear about Kerrville?" It was Norma Sue.

Cassie nodded, then realized she had to speak. "Yes, Norma Sue. I heard the news."

"Do you think they'll call Junior back?" Leave it to Norma Sue to raise the specter of Junior returning to the Texas Rangers.

Cassie suppressed a desire to smash the phone. How dare Norma Sue call herself a friend. "Junior promised. I'm not worried." She desperately wanted to end the conversation. "Uh-oh, Norma Sue, I smell some biscuits burning. Bye," she said and hung up the phone. She braced herself for a moment against the table, just staring at the phone. Junior would never renege on a promise. She felt sure of that. Pretty much. That polished relic from his brief tour as a Texas Ranger still sat in the top drawer of the dresser. It was now a memento, not something to ever pin on his shirt again. Yes, a polished relic of the past.

The stillness was broken by the sound of hoofbeats. A rider was coming in hard and fast. Horse and rider pulled up in a cloud of dust in front of the house, and Cassie heard the clomp of boots and jingle of spurs as the rider bounded up the gallery stairs. The expected knock on the door followed.

"Who is it?" she asked from inside. Just in case, she grasped the Colt revolver from the stand beside the door.

"Johnnie Crockett, ma'am. I have a message for Mr. Dunn."

Cassie released the hammer of the Colt and laid it back on the table. She opened the door to a hard-breathing young man with a sealed envelope in his hand. The visitor was young, not more than fifteen. He had a shock of blond hair but no facial whiskers yet.

"Mr. Dunn is inspecting some cattle. How may I help you?"

Crockett handed her the envelope. "I've been asked to be sure that Mr. Dunn gets this."

"I'll be certain to give it to him, Johnnie." She now recalled having seen the young man at church. "Would you care for some water or coffee?"

Crockett shook his head gratefully. "I'll water my horse and be on my way, if you don't mind, ma'am," he said as he turned about, bounded down the stairs, and led his cayuse to the water trough.

Cassie held the envelope to her breast. What news might it bring? She knew better than to open it, but it was mighty tempting. She hoped I would be back soon enough to ease her curiosity.

The black-clad figure stood on the highest bluff. Its rough-hewn rocky face cascaded about thirty feet to the river below. The mist rising from the meandering waters below glowed hauntingly in the starlight. The man scanned the far bank as though awaiting a signal. He squinted to better try to penetrate the mists. He felt a chill even though the moist air was warm.

He heard a boot scrape on rocks somewhere behind him. A loosened pebble tumbled down the trail. Urgency crept into his thinking. Someone was coming up the path to his position. The footsteps came ever nearer. He heard labored breathing.

"Gordon?" whispered a voice from the darkness. The visitor was but a few yards away and had reached the edge of the cliff overlooking the river.

Gordon took a final look across the river. Where was the signal? But for the mist, Gordon might have seen the crouched figure on the opposite bank bring the barrel of the Winchester up. The rushing waters masked the sound of the lever action. He couldn't have seen the eyes aiming or the finger squeezing the trigger. He did see a small burst of light. It was the last thing he'd see on this earth. A bullet passed through his chest. He never heard the blast from the rifle's muzzle, as he collapsed dead before he hit the ground. His momentum pitched him over the cliff. His body quickly disappeared in the flowing currents of the Guadalupe River.

The visitor slinked back down the trail, muttering, "I tried to warn yuh, Gordon. Damn, but I tried." He mounted a horse and disappeared into the night. Who had killed his friend? Who had warned him? Sheriff John Vann rode hard away from the scene. He felt so out of his element. His job as a tax collector was far easier than being sheriff. Would the help he'd requested come in time?

★★

"Terrible weather," I observed as I entered the kitchen and gave Cassie a loving kiss.

"Eww, you're wet, Lucas."

"You'll dry off, my love won't," I said with a laugh and kissed her again.

What could she say? Dinner was just about ready. A steaming beef stew would take the edge from my rain-dampened hide. "Grab some coffee and sit, Lucas."

Soon enough, she delivered a bowl of piping-hot stew before me.

I took a sip of coffee and smiled appreciatively. "South range is in good shape. We counted two hundred and seventy head." We'd been raising the Santa Gertrudis breed acquired from the King Ranch to the south. These beeves packed on nearly twice the meat as the longhorns they used to raise at Heaven's Gate. "How was your day, sweetheart?"

"Got a call from Norma Sue. She can be right annoying at times."

I feared I was about to get an earful of gossip. "She seems to always know who is doing what to whom," I blurted. "I think they call that gossip." Cassie's expression dissuaded me of that line of thought.

"She asked me whether you'd be called back to the Texas Rangers to solve the goings on in Kerrville."

"What did you tell her?" I asked.

"That you promised you'd never go back. She flustered me, so I made an excuse and hung up." Cassie was visibly upset.

I thought back on how my father had hung up his Texas Ranger badge with a promise to my mother. Then, threatening circumstances caused her to release him from the promise. I wondered whether such a thing could happen between me and Cassie. I washed down a morsel of stew with a long sip of coffee. "What set her to ask such a question, sweetheart?"

"This," responded Cassie, as she handed the envelope to me. "That blabbermouth messenger!"

"Telegram for me?"

"The messenger rode hard from Nuecestown to deliver it. Must be important." Given that many messages languished at the telegraph office for days awaiting delivery, the apparent urgency of this one deeply concerned Cassie.

I tore the envelope open and pulled the telegram free. I slowly unfolded it, read it, and reread it before tentatively handing it to Cassie.

"You're not?" she looked deeply into my eyes.

The polished silver badge in the top drawer of the dresser was calling. Its voice came loudly to my ears. I sighed. "Guess a promise is a promise," I said with all-too-obvious reluctance.

It was plain to Cassie where my heart lay. I was my father's son, the son of a legendary Texas Ranger. We weren't hurting for money, as Heaven's Gate had been good to us the past year or so. We didn't need the meager Texas Ranger pay. Captain Hughes's telegram had a pleading tone, yet he knew that Texas Ranger blood flowed deep in my veins. Once a Texas Ranger, always a Texas Ranger, was embedded in Hughes's message. He just wanted me to look into the murders on the Guadalupe River in Kerrville and help Sheriff Vann where I could. She stared across the table, searching my eyes. She loved me so much. My very soul had become an open book to her. No secrets were hidden. She nodded.

"Are you?" I cocked my head questioningly.

"I love you, Lucas Dunn Junior." She sighed. "I'd never stand between you and your passion for the law." Love flowed from her being as she paused. "You stay away from gunplay." She knew better but had to say it. "I want you back here to help raise our children." She arose slowly and headed for the bedroom.

I watched her with wonder. Cassie McCully Dunn was one very special woman. She'd have done well as a woman of the frontier. I heard her soft steps and felt her approach me from behind.

Cassie reached her arms around and pinned the Texas Ranger badge on my shirt. She swept around to face me and admire her work. "Now, you look like a Texas Ranger, Lucas," she said with a loving smile tinged with a hint of bittersweetness.

I stood and wrapped my arms around her, burying her in my chest. "I'll be careful," I said as though it needed saying. Careful was an easy word to say.

"Mother invited us to dinner on Sunday. Do you think Sheriff Vann can wait a few days?"

I nodded. "Guess he has no choice. I better ride into town tomorrow and send a telegram to Captain Hughes."

FIVE
LINGERING QUESTIONS

I RODE EASY-LIKE INTO KERRVILLE. The place was a bustling hub of trade these days. Most folks traveled by horse or wagon. I'd heard of something called a horse-less carriage, but that was back east. I felt quite at home in the saddle. Besides, a horse could go just about any place necessary.

Asking questions of a couple of passersby on the main street, I found my way to the jail, erstwhile office of tax collector and Sheriff John William Vann. I was about to dismount and hitch Tornado when a young man leaning back in a chair on the wooden-plank sidewalk raised the brim of his hat. "You lookin' fer Sheriff Vann?"

I paused my dismount. "Yes. Yes I am."

"He be down yonder," he said with a finger pointing toward the Guadalupe River a couple of hundred yards from where we stood.

"Much obliged. He fishing?" I asked.

"In a manner of speakin'." The young man offered a wry grin. "Floater found this mornin'."

"Another killing?" I asked pretty much rhetorically.

The young man nodded.

I headed for the river and soon found Sheriff Vann taking notes as he stood over a body dragged up on the riverbank. I ground-hitched Tornado and worked my way down the embankment toward Vann. Two men, likely there as witnesses or helping the coroner, gave me a once-over. I made sure that my Texas Ranger badge was visible. "Sheriff Vann?" I called.

Vann paused his pencil and looked up from his notes. "You the fellow Captain Hughes said he'd send?" He looked again then did a double-take. "You're Luke Dunn's boy, aren't you?"

"Yes sir. Texas Ranger Lucas Dunn Junior."

"You solved that vigilante case, didn't you?" asked Vann.

"Matter of fact," I said with a sheepish grin and likely a slight blush. Notoriety wasn't my forte.

"When we're done here, we'll head back to my office and I'll share what we've learned so far. Like to find where this fellow was shot, too. I've got a hunch it was just a ways up the river."

I nodded. "I'm at your service, Sheriff."

Vann sighed resignedly. "Been trying to link the pieces of these killings together. Can't help feeling this is bigger than Kerr County, Junior. Er...do you mind me calling you Junior?"

"No problem, Sheriff." I took a gander at the body. The water-logged skin shrouded in the paleness of death had a certain peacefulness despite its life having ended in violence. "You say you have an idea as to where this occurred?"

Vann hung his head. "Truth be told, I was there. Tried to warn Gordon here."

Curiosity suddenly aroused, I gave Vann a penetrating

stare. "How come you were on the scene? Did you know something?"

Vann looked away. "Someone left me a note." He sighed deeply. "Obviously, I was too late."

I scratched my chin and chewed on that tidbit of information. "Sounds as though you've got a mysterious informer. Maybe whomever is responsible for the murders has a spy in his midst."

"Or someone with a conscience," added Vann. The sheriff motioned to the two men standing nearby. "I'm done here. Y'all can take the body. I'll contact Mrs. Wilson."

I watched the two men hoist the dead man's body onto a blanket and begin to drag it up the hill from the riverbank.

"Long as we're here, let me show you the murder scene, Junior." Vann took a final look at where the body had laid and led the way up the hill. "We can cross over upstream a bit. My horse is over yonder."

On the way upriver, Vann gave me an overview of the evidence he'd collected thus far. It was a lot, but not much. There was nothing to identify a killer, no names, no associations, no known threats of any size big enough to set off multiple murders. Whomever was at its root cause was committed to destroying any evidence other than bullet casings. It didn't take long to scope the murder scene. Vann pointed to a spot across the river from the bluff upon which Gordon Wilson had stood. "See those bushes over beyond that tall cypress?"

I nodded. "That's about a hundred and fifty yards, Sheriff. The killer's a pretty fair marksman."

"Likely so, but there's no shortage of good shots around these parts," rejoined Vann. "Plenty of hunters."

"You been over there?" I asked.

"Yep. Found a single casing. Likely from one of those 1895 Winchester rifles. Caliber would fit. Lots of Winchesters around."

I nodded. "The vigilante I caught used a Winchester, so I appreciate the dilemma, Sheriff."

"Let's head back to my office, and we can go over what I've got," Vann said.

"Just to be sure. You have no idea who warned you of the intention to kill Wilson?"

"Anonymous," Vann assured me.

I mounted Tornado and followed Vann. A nettlesome concern had begun to form. How did Vann know to warn the latest victim? What did the sheriff know that he wasn't revealing? The idea of the sheriff having been left a warning note seemed flimsy.

We rode back in silence, as I pondered what I'd learned thus far. There was no point in advancing theories just yet. The word mystery hung large over the situation. In fact, it was more like mysteries. There was a lot yet to root out. For one thing, a motive had yet to rear its ugly head.

I examined Vann's meager gathering of evidence. Shell casings weren't much to go on. Two of the victims had been plugged with a small caliber weapon, likely a pocket pistol similar to a Derringer. Whomever that murderer was, had to have been a crack shot even at close range. Then there was the question of the victims shot with the rifle, likely a larger caliber akin to the 1895 Winchester that I carried. There were far too many of those rifles around to link one with the bushwhacker. Likely, a third firearm was involved with the victim found near the canoe. Five bodies and three guns was a tad overwhelming. There must be a link somewhere, but it wasn't leaping out. I had a hunch that three of the victims were killed to silence them as potential witnesses.

"So, you've only been able to identify Gordon Wilson and Sam Waltz?" I asked.

Vann nodded.

"Mind if I start nosing around town?" I reckoned to do so anyway, but it was respectful to ask. I didn't want the sheriff to think I would keep him unaware of my investigations.

Vann smiled. "Go ahead. Best of luck. Folks who might know anything are tighter than a saddle cinch. A few unexplained killings will tend to do that to folks."

"I'll let you know if I find anything worthwhile."

SIX
CONNECTING DOTS

IN SOME WAYS, the old west lingered on in Kerrville. Ranches still abounded, but barbed wire had divided the land. That didn't mean the region was any more civilized than places like Alice or Galveston, but it remained a bit of a throwback to years long past despite pushing toward a population of nearly three thousand five hundred. While folks strolled the streets regularly, any meaningful community information was exchanged at local watering holes. I reckoned it to be a logical place to start snooping for leads.

There was a saloon up the street from the jailhouse. A couple of horses were hitched out front. I reckoned it was testament to the midday hour that there wouldn't be many folks imbibing. It was a nondescript place. Most folks would likely call it shabby. I shrugged and walked through a pair of swinging doors.

It took a few seconds for my eyes to adjust to the dimness. There were a half dozen tables, including one occupied by the cowboys to whom the horses hitched outside belonged. I nodded toward them and made my way to the bar. There were a couple of saloons in Kerrville, and I wasn't going to get myself drunk drinking at each.

The barkeep gave me an inquisitive look.

"A beer, thanks," I said.

As he walked over with beer in hand, he noticed the Texas Ranger badge on my shirt. "You here fer them killings?" he said. The look in his eyes said he was craving juicy information that nobody else would know.

I smiled politely and ambled over to the table beside the cowboys. I sat and placed my hat crown down next to my beer. The men appeared to be honest, hard-working cowboys taking a break from whatever brought them to Kerrville. Both wore the chaps and spurs that were trademarks of their craft.

"Howdy. I'm Chet and my pard here is Slim. Couldn't help but hear the barkeep. You here 'bout them killings?" asked Chet with an inquisitive expression.

I smiled. "My name's Dunn. Yes, I'm here to investigate the recent murders."

Chet's eyes widened. "You kin of that Texas Ranger Luke Dunn?"

I nodded. It seemed this was a cross of sorts that I'd always bear. Actually, I was right proud that he was so well thought of.

Slim took a long sip of his beer and sized me up through squinty eyes. "I think them killings are hooked up with that Kilkenny fella. He's buyin' up all sorts of land 'round these parts. He be close to Archer Parr."

I tried not to flinch at the Parr name. I'd already had a taste of him after solving the vigilante case. "You seem to know more than most folks, Slim."

"Overheard our foreman talkin' with the boss man 'bout an offer Kilkenny made. Hear tell boss man be fearin' fer his life."

"Most any wrangler 'round these parts gonna tell yuh the same, Ranger Dunn," chimed in Chet.

"Kilkenny has money?" I asked pretty much rhetorically.

Both cowboys nodded.

"Where might I find this Kilkenny fellow?" I inquired.

Chet laughed. "Not here fer sure."

"He's got a place west of town," said Slim.

The barkeep walked over and set a second beer before me. "On the house, Ranger. Folks worry 'bout headin' out near the river these days. Hope yuh can change that."

"Thanks kindly," I responded.

The barkeep smiled. "Figured to save yuh a trip to other saloons. Yer gonna hear the same story."

So, I was right about where to go to learn the local theory about the murders and possible motive. I made up my mind to pay this Kilkenny fellow a visit. Might be good to get acquainted, and I could play the game from my own Stephen Powers and Archer Parr deck. "This Kilkenny fellow live here long?"

"Joseph Kilkenny come to these parts from Galveston. Word has it, he got rich shippin' goods 'round the world."

I nodded. It was a familiar story. Man becomes wealthy and looks to leverage his wealth into other ventures. There was likely a certain allure to becoming a big-time rancher in Texas. Nevertheless, this was coming together far too easily. Vann could have easily figured this out. What piece or pieces was I missing? I took a long swallow of beer. "Much obliged for the information, gents." I pushed back and stood. "Reckon I'll have a chat with this Kilkenny fellow." I figured word would get out that a Texas Ranger was looking for the man long before I actually visited him. Besides, I wanted to see what Vann's thinking might be.

★★

It turned out that Vann was aware of Kilkenny's land predations but didn't figure him to be a killer or even inclined to hire folks to do that sort of work. I sure didn't reckon Vann to be the naïve sort so I respected his perspective on the man. Still, if Kilkenny wasn't behind the killings, who could it be?

I saddled Tornado and headed to Kilkenny's spread. As I came within sight of the gateway arch at the entrance, I couldn't miss the cowhand setting on a bench alongside his cayuse. News of my planned visit hadn't taken long to reach Kilkenny's ears.

"You must be Texas Ranger Dunn," inquired the cowboy, as his eyes riveted in on my badge.

I nodded. "It appears that Mr. Kilkenny is expecting me."

"Seems like," responded the hand with a knowing smile. "Normally, we ask guests to leave their weapons in yonder box, but since you're a lawman, that won't be necessary."

He was letting me know that security was an issue. As I rode on through the gate, I scanned the horizon. Vann mentioned that Kilkenny owned around fifty thousand acres and was trying to buy up surrounding spreads. It was pretty country. I noted that the brand was depicted on the arch with a large Bar K symbol made of iron. I chuckled to myself that it would be an easy brand for rustlers to alter with a running iron.

We rode silently for close to a mile before reaching a comfortable-looking ranch house. There was nothing the least ostentatious about the place that might hint at a very wealthy owner. I noticed a row of a half dozen wagons off to one side along a trail leading to a stable. It gave me pause to wonder what business other than shipping Kilkenny might be in? We reined in.

"I'll let Mr. Kilkenny know you're here," said my escort. He dismounted and knocked on the ranch house door.

I heard some noises from inside and the muffled sound of a voice.

"Wait here. Mr. Kilkenny will be out in a moment," advised my escort who proceeded to mount up and head toward the stable.

There I sat astride Tornado. The sun was high, and it was getting right warm. Tornado pawed at the ground impatiently.

Finally, the door opened. A young woman appeared. "Ranger Dunn?" she asked, knowing full well who I was.

"Yes, ma'am," I responded.

"It's miss, and please come in," she said in a voice smooth as silk. She stood with the door open behind her and motioned me in.

It was all I could do to keep my jaw from falling agape. She was nearly as beautiful as Cassie. Long, curly raven locks cascaded below her shoulders and framed deep brown eyes and perfectly formed lips. I slid from my saddle and tied Tornado's reins to an ornate iron-hitching post. I did this slowly so as to gather my wits at this unexpected turn.

"My father is in the library," she said and pointed down a wide corridor. So, Kilkenny had a daughter.

I'd already realized that the house layout was deceptive in that it was far larger than it appeared from the front. John Kilkenny was of the monied folk for sure. The door to the library was open. I entered to the pungent aroma of cigar smoke. He must have been smoking for a while, as there was a haze that dimmed the light from two windows at the far end of the room. Two of the walls were taken over by shelves overflowing with books. "Mistuh Dunn?" a gravely voice wafted from behind a huge oak desk bedecked with intricate carvings.

As I approached, Kilkenny swung his leather uphol-stered swivel chair around to face me. "Yes, Mr. Kilkenny. I'm Texas Ranger Luke Dunn." I waited for the inevitable question. It came.

"Are you kin to the famed Texas Ranger?"

"My father, sir."

He nodded and motioned to the leather-bound chair beside the desk. "Cigar?" He lifted a wooden box and offered me a smoke.

"Thanks, but no." I waved off the smoke.

"Surely you'll enjoy coffee?"

"Thanks, I'd love some."

"Diana," he called. "Kindly fetch this gentleman a cup of coffee."

"I don't want to be any trouble, sir."

Kilkenny winked. "My daughter is bored to tears and brewing coffee will give her something to do," he whis-pered with his hand aside his mouth.

"You have an impressive library, Mr. Kilkenny."

"I do enjoy a good book now and again." He took a long pull on the cigar and laid it beside an ashtray. He folded his hands and leaned forward. "So, what brings you here, Ranger Dunn?"

I was about to reply, when Diana strolled in and placed a cup of steaming hot coffee before me. "Sugar, Mr. Dunn?" she asked with an ever-so-sweet silken voice.

"Thanks, but I'll take it straight," I said with a cordial smile.

She returned my smile and glided from the library as if swept away on a cloud.

I turned to Kilkenny. "Captain Hughes sent me to help

Sheriff Vann investigate the recent murders on the river. My gut tells me they're connected, but I'm searching for a motive in hopes of finding who is behind them."

Kilkenny relit his cigar and leaned back in his chair. "What sort of motive might drive men to such foul deeds, Ranger Dunn?"

"Most often around these parts, it involves land." I let that drop and awaited his reaction.

Kilkenny nodded. "Land. It is often acquired honestly." His implication that he'd never resort to dishonest or threatening methods was clear.

"I hear tell we have a common acquaintance with Archer Parr."

"Ah, you know Archie? Good man that one. Going places for sure. Maybe governor someday." Kilkenny waxed fondly about Parr. "How did you connect with him?"

"I was wrapping up some Texas Ranger business in Brownsville and met Stephen Powers. He led me to Mr. Parr." I didn't mention that I judged Parr to be the very embodiment of a power-hungry politician who'd stoop at nothing to gain and hold influence for financial gain.

"Arch helped me find this spread," added Kilkenny. "Real bargain this one."

I wondered how much of a bargain and whether Kilkenny owed Parr any favors. "Archer Parr is holding right-big sway down near Corpus Christi." I let that state-ment sort of hang out there for Kilkenny to grab. I was beginning to see Archer Parr as a man who would use whatever means necessary to achieve his ends. Violence and corruption headed my list as tools of Parr's ambitions.

"You don't think I had anything to do with these goings on down at the Guadalupe?" Kilkenny said with a hurt expression plastered across his face.

I thoughtfully glanced at the shelves loaded with books then looked back at the man. "I'm a long way from drawing conclusions, Mr. Kilkenny. I'd heard that you were seeking to purchase more land around Kerrville and reckoned to judge for myself whether you are an honest broker."

"And?" he asked in a challenging tone.

I took a long sip of coffee. "What do you think?" It was an impertinent response.

Kilkenny took a long drag on his cigar and exhaled a puff of smoke skyward. "I'm sure you're aware that I run a large shipping business based in Galveston. I've got plenty of money." The clear implication was that he had no rational reason to threaten anyone into selling land, much less being involved in murders.

He made sense. I looked over at the wall opposite the bookcases. "Those are impressive, Mr. Kilkenny," I said, pointing to a pair of bull elk trophy heads that seemed large enough to tilt the wall.

Kilkenny replied with a proud smile. "Those? My daughter bagged them. The one on the left at a good four hundred yards. She's bagged a big horn and a mountain lion, too."

That was an interesting tidbit. The petite, delicate daughter was a capable hunter of big game. I tried to picture her in the wilds, sighting down the barrel of a big-bore rifle.

"Impressive," I nodded.

Just then, Diana knocked and tip-toed into the room. "Care for more coffee, Mr. Dunn?" she asked in that same sweet-as-sugar voice.

"I do thank you, Miss Kilkenny, but I must be going." I stood and smiled congenially.

She nodded and turned to her father.

Kilkenny smiled and seemed to relax upon her entrance.

"You're welcome to borrow a book or two, Ranger Dunn," he offered. With that, he lifted himself awkwardly from his chair, and with the help of a walking stick, limped over to a bookshelf. He perused the shelf for a moment, pulled two books, blew a little dust from them, and handed the volumes to me. "You might enjoy these," he said with earnest eyes.

"Thanks kindly, Mr. Kilkenny."

"Diana, please show Texas Ranger Dunn to the door. It was a pleasure meeting you. You're welcome here anytime. I don't get out so much lately. Perhaps, we could discuss those books." He gestured to the two books he'd shared with me and motioned Diana and me toward the library door.

I followed her down the hallway to the front door. She seemed to glide rather than walk. I couldn't help but note that she cut a right-fine figure. "Your father seems lonely, Miss Kilkenny," I observed in an attempt to make conversation.

"You may call me Diana, Ranger Dunn." She gave me a half curtsy that revealed the ample swell of breasts pushed up against her bodice. "My Father has had a rough few weeks since a horse kicked his leg," she added with a demure smile.

Before I could check myself, I said, "You can call me Lucas." I felt the warmth of a blush sweep up my neck. "Er...nice to meet you, Miss...Diana."

I couldn't move fast enough to be on Tornado and away from the Bar K Ranch. I thought I might be connecting some dots as to motive, but I wasn't convinced that Kilkenny was clear. I needed hard evidence.

SEVEN
MYSTERIES ABOUND

"HAVE you been able to identify any victims beside Gordon Wilson and Sam Waltz?" I asked Sheriff Vann. I'd just given him a summary of my meeting with Kilkenny, though I held back my suspicions of his possible nefarious links with Archer Parr. He agreed that the jury was still out as to whether the shipping magnate had any involvement.

"The two likely killed with a small-bore pocket pistol were Pete and Wiley Tolliver. They were local ne'er-do-wells known to take odd jobs around Kerrville and up around Fredericksburg. The dead man near Waltz's body alongside the canoe was a man known to frequent San Antonio named Charlie Hawks. Hawks and the Tollivers were all guns for hire, as I understand it. I have a poster on him saying he was wanted in Nuevo Laredo for killing a man in a card game. By my thinking, one of the Tollivers shot Waltz, dragged him to the river bank, and plopped him into the canoe at Hawks's direction. Hawks then killed them to dispose of witnesses then headed downstream with Waltz's body. Someone decided to eliminate Hawks." Vann paused to let this all sink in with me and to gather his thoughts. "It all seemed right tidy until the next night when Wilson was murdered. Waltz and Wilson both owned parcels of lush grazing pasture north and west of Kerrville."

"Do you think land acquisition was the motive?" I asked.

"Almost too simple, isn't it?" Vann postulated.

I stroked my chin thoughtfully. "I've got a hunch that our killer will lay low for a bit. You've been a lawman long enough to know that when crime comes too easy, the evil-doers tend to get careless. I'm of a mind that this killer isn't stupid. He's tied up loose ends so far as he's concerned."

"I'll keep an eye on who shows up to grab the Wilson and Waltz spreads."

I nodded. "You can be sure that it won't be our killer."

I set off to familiarize myself with the region. I wondered what properties contiguous to the Wilson and Waltz parcels and even Kilkenny's might be especially attractive. Heavy on my mind was that they were apparently worth killing for.

Before heading out, I figured to resupply. If there was a killer on the loose somewhere out there—and likely a professional—I dared not be unprepared. I saddled Tornado and headed toward Crocker's Ranch & Trail Goods, an establishment a ways up the street from the jail.

I slid from my saddle, hitched Tornado to the rail in front of the store, and bounded up a couple of steps to a wooden-plank walkway that ran across the front of the store. Unfortunately, I had my head down. As I reached the walkway, I was brought up short by a strong whiff of perfume and the top of a lady's hat. I'd nearly bowled over

Diana Kilkenny. I backed off a half step. "Sorry, ma'am," I blurted.

"It's Diana. And no apologies necessary, Mr. Texas Ranger," she delivered with a smile that could have melted glaciers.

"Er...good to see you, Diana. Sorry to nearly knock you over."

"But you stopped just close enough," she cooed. She batted her eyes and eased past me to a nearby bay gelding. She deposited some purchases in the saddlebags.

Somehow—and first impressions often being misguided—I hadn't envisioned her out and about riding horses. As she had strode—or rather glided—to her mount, I couldn't help but notice that she wore riding britches. They fit her right well.

Diana mounted and gave me a curious look. "Come join us for dinner, Lucas." She didn't wait for an answer, but turned the gelding. "We eat at six," she said over her shoulder and spurred away.

I was left dumbfounded. She was one very attractive woman. Pangs of guilt swept over me, as I thought on Cassie. I entered the shop with my mind a conflicting mix of wanting to know more of the Kilkenny's but avoiding Diana's quite obvious charms.

I purchased some ammunition and beef jerky for the trail. Deep in my heart, I knew that I'd be ending my day at the Kilkenny's. I tried to shake away the image of Diana, but it hung there like sticker burrs to bare feet. I was being drawn in. My father had warned that if you reckoned to avoid the heat, stay away from the fire. Maybe this fire was a tad too hot.

★★

Who was the killer who'd disposed of Hawks and Wilson, assuming there was a single shooter? Whomever he was, he specialized in bushwhacking. If I could find the killer, I might be able to figure who had paid him. On the other hand, I might find the person who'd hired the killer, unless they were one and the same. Mysteries were abounding. I shook my head as if to clear it while guiding Tornado over the rugged hills and wide ranchlands around Kerrville. I visited the Guadalupe a couple of times in my wanderings to water Tornado and rest my bones. My travels were giving me plenty of time to try to sort things out.

I decided to accept Diana's dinner offer. She made no bones about her interest in me, but I was confident that I could fend off her intentions while learning more about the Kilkennys. I headed Tornado up the trail toward the Bar K Ranch.

The ranch gate was set wide open. Now, there was an invitation. I began to feel like a fly approaching the web of a black widow spider. I pulled up. Tornado whinnied and bobbed his head. It seemed he wasn't so sure of this little adventure either.

Guess I was resigned to my fate, as I nudged Tornado forward.

Window candles cast a warm glow around the perimeter of the house. The appearance of the place oozed wealth even in the dim light. I gazed up at a clear sky filled with stars and crowned by a nearly full moon.

I slid from my saddle and hitched Tornado at the post. Hitching my belt, I turned to see Diana leaning against a gallery post and taking me in with her deep brown eyes. Her dress was designed to bring full attention to her well-endowed chest. She had an aura of self-assurance that said she was satisfied that she'd lured me into her web. "Good evening, Diana," I said as calmly as I could. I hoped she couldn't see my knees trembling. It was all I could do to keep my eyes from her breasts.

"Why Lucas, how nice of you to accept my invitation," she cooed with a winsome smile. "Do come in." She led the way into the parlor. Her dress swayed alluringly over her slim hips.

I hung my hat on a post as I stepped into the foyer. My premonition of stepping into a spider web seemed all too real.

Diana glanced down at my gun. "I don't think you'll be needing that this evening, Mr. Texas Ranger," said the spider to the fly.

I smiled sort of sheepishly, unbuckled my belt, and hung gun and holster on a post provided for that purpose. Diana beckoned me toward the dining room, and I followed like a cayuse on a tether.

The dining room was empty save for a Black server. "Where's your father?" I ventured hopefully.

"He was tired and turned in early," she replied with sugar-coated sweetness. "It will be just the two of us. I look forward to learning more of you, Lucas."

Her phrasing put me on high alert. Her wanting to know more *of* me rather than *about* me seemed an invitation to disaster—mine.

"Please sit," she offered as the server pulled back a chair for her.

I sat, and without further ado, another server began placing plates heaped with fine cuisine before us. Another filled our goblets with red wine.

The candles between us bathed her face in a delicious warmth. I hadn't as yet lifted a fork or knife nor sipped the wine.

"Do feel free to eat, Lucas," she urged with a flirting batting of her eyes.

I didn't know which to avoid staring at, her eyes or her breasts. I scooped a forkful of peas and spilled them on my plate as I felt her foot rub against the shank of my boot.

"Think fast," I told myself. "Er, my boot is clean, Diana." Talk about a mood breaker. She yanked her foot back and sat up primly.

"So, any clues as to the shootings?" she asked.

There wasn't much I was up to sharing. "We have a pretty good idea of the sequence of the killings."

"Well," she began with an indignant tone. "There've been five folks killed. Is that the best a Texas Ranger can do?"

"I've been here three days, Diana. There's more, but I'm afraid I can't discuss all I've learned."

She sighed and began to slide back into her flirtatious role. I say role, because it was clearly a contrived act. She knew I was a husband and father, yet was using her wiles to milk me for what I knew. I hadn't yet figured out why she was so interested. She surely wasn't interdicting on behalf of her father, as he was a tough old nut with plenty of experience at intrigue, whether in life or business. "You won't share with little me?" she asked. Her foot ventured forward again.

I managed to dodge this come-on by shifting in the chair and pulling my feet back. "What was your mother like?" I asked—another mood breaker.

Her eyes pointed to a painting on the wall.

I gathered it was of her mother. "She was a beautiful woman," I offered up.

"She passed away giving birth to me." A sadness swept her face for a second then reverted to the flirtatious persona she's taken on.

I was relieved when the servers brought out slices of cherry pie with ice cream. I half expected coffee, but a glass of what appeared to be whiskey was placed before each of us. I figured it was a fine whiskey, but I wasn't about to have my senses dulled in any way. I took a tiny sip to be cordial.

Diana savored a fragment of pie lingering on her lips. A little melted ice cream ran down her chin, and she promptly licked it away with a sexy swipe of her tongue. She gave me a dreamy look and quaffed the whiskey in a single gulp. A server quickly refilled her glass. Between the wine and now the whiskey affecting any inhibitions, I reckoned she'd soon be even looser with her charms. Red warning flags unfurled in my mind.

Dinner was finally over. She'd eaten half of her dessert but imbibed at least four glasses of the whiskey. She stood and tipped slightly forward. I feared her breasts might fall from her bodice. "Care for a nightcap?" she murmured, as she regained her balance.

"I've got a long day tomorrow, Diana. Best I be heading out."

She laid a decidedly disappointed look on me with pouted lips. "Oh, Lucas," she purred. "It's early." She batted her eyes. As we walked toward the door to the parlor, she swept in front of me, reached an arm around my neck, and thrust her ample chest into mine. Her full crimson lips sought mine.

I felt the eyes of the woman in the painting bore down upon me from its lofty perch. I turned my head and managed a cough. It was a relief to come up with still another mood breaker.

Diana stepped back just enough that I was able to grab my gun belt from the peg. Her hand ran down my chest as I strapped the rig around my hips. "My!" she exclaimed softly. "Your muscles seem to have muscles, Lucas." Her hand was headed lower.

I was able to reach over her and grab my hat. Admittedly, my manhood was coming to attention, as her hand found its way to my crotch. There was no doubt whatsoever as to her intentions. My, but she was a tempting woman... seductive...tantalizing...enticing.

Her efforts were straining at the shackles of my resistance—at my fear of being caught in her web. She knew it full well.

I was desperate to escape. If I'd lingered another moment in the parlor, I might have succumbed. "Thank you for a lovely evening," I offered and broke free of her wayward hand, of the sticky mesh of her all-entrapping web.

I couldn't get to Tornado fast enough. As it was, my erect manhood didn't make the walk especially comfortable. My instincts told me that there was something about this entire evening that wasn't ringing true, but I wasn't able to figure it out just yet. She was a woman determined to get whatever she wanted by any means necessary. This case was becoming ever-more-complicated, as its mysteries abounded.

EIGHT
WOMAN SCORNED?

AS I OPENED my hotel room door, a note fluttered to the ground. I unfolded it and was not totally surprised to read a threat.

> GO NEAR DTANA KILKENNY AGAIN
> AND YOU WILL DIE

That was surely an attention-getter. Was there a jealous suitor out there? Perhaps, it was an angry father? I examined the note more closely. In fact, I sensed the sweet aroma of perfume. I looked at the neatly written words again. Could a woman have written them? These were angry, threatening words. If a man had written them, I would have expected a bolder hand even penetrating the paper. Nope. I reckoned this note was from a scorned woman, a woman frustrated at my not succumbing to her charms. I folded it and stored it in a pocket inside my saddlebags with other notes about the case.

This was already figuring to be an interesting day. I

planned to meet briefly with Sheriff Vann before going back to the saloon circuit to learn what I could. Kerrville was certainly full of surprises, and I'd barely skimmed the surface of possibilities. The big remaining question was who profited from the deaths of Wilson and Waltz? Who would now own their land holdings? Since Vann was also tax collector, I figured he should know.

Vann was pouring through a stack of papers at his desk when I strode into his office. "Morning, Sheriff."

"I've been wondering what you've found out, Junior," he said with a mischievous smile. "Enjoy dinner?"

I wondered if everyone knew that I'd dined at the Kilkenny's ranch. "I escaped with my scalp," I said with an attempt at humor.

"Diana's quite a woman," Vann observed and leaned back in his chair. "You look like you have a question ready to bust from your tongue."

"Did Wilson and Waltz have heirs to their holdings?"

"Hmmm. Good question, Ranger." Vann got up and strode to an adjoining room. He squatted before a file cabinet, opened the bottom drawer, and rifled through some files. He emerged with two files. "Convenient that both names begin with the same letter," he noted while rubbing his back. He examined the file contents and shook his head. "Nothing here."

"Could there be wills?"

"You'll have to check the courthouse about that. I vaguely recall that Wilson was a widower and had no children. Don't know about Waltz."

"Point me to the courthouse," I responded. I was about to head out, when I recalled the threatening note. "By the way, I received a note this morning to stay away from Diana Kilkenny. She have a suitor?"

Vann laughed. "Every man in Kerrville would like to bed that filly. No telling who might have left you a note."

"After I visit the courthouse, I'm fixing to head back home for a couple of days to tend to some personal business. This case doesn't look as though it will be solved overnight. I wont' be long." I shook my head at Vann's response to the note and headed to the courthouse. Given her flirtatious manners, it would be no surprise that Diana must have quite a reputation around Kerrville.

I considered hanging around until Sunday and attending the church Diana was known to frequent. That would be a sure opportunity to overhear gossipy women talking about her wiles. It didn't take me long to reckon that was a lousy reason to go to church and would only serve to confirm what I'd already figured.

The courthouse didn't turn out to be especially helpful. Vann was right that Wilson had no heirs, so his estate would go to a condition that was termed intestate. This meant that Texas would decide how his assets would be distributed. Waltz did have a will, but the clerk confided that it hadn't been updated and the designated heir had passed on. Thus, the estates of both men were bathed in uncertainty. They'd surely be ripe for acquisition. There was no telling who might wind up with the property, though intuition had me leaning to Kilkenny or possibly Archer Parr. I had no solid evidence as yet, just some suspicions that were circumstantial at best. I decided to let these facts percolate, while I headed for Nuecestown.

In preparing for my journey home, I came upon the two books Kilkenny had loaned me. I'd absentmindedly shoved them into my saddlebags and forgotten them. Now, I held *Huckleberry Finn* by a fellow named Mark Twain and *Red Badge of Courage* by Stephen Crane in my hands. I flipped through the pages and decided to read the Crane book first, as its title intrigued me. Reading would surely make the hours on the trail pass more quickly. Besides, I was curious as to why Kilkenny had chosen those two books to loan to me.

I bade farewell to Sheriff Vann, assuring him that I'd return in a couple of weeks.

Well, the journey from Kerrville to Nuecestown on horseback was a weeklong endeavor. In addition to being alert to the dangers still part of a frontier that was rapidly disappearing, I managed to read *Red Badge of Courage*. It offered a perspective on the War Between the States that my growing up in Texas had insulated me from. It was the tale of a young recruit who learns of the cruelties of war. While the descriptions of conflict were vivid and delved into the inner workings of the main character's mind, it seemed to me that the author had never been in battle himself. I was nearly home, when I finished reading. I wondered what message, if any, that Kilkenny was trying to deliver to me. Perhaps, it was about the impact of violence on the human psyche. A warning? Simply advice? I determined that I'd have to discuss it with the man himself. I sighed and reckoned I'd save *Huckleberry Finn* for my return to Kerrville. The experience got me to realizing that I needed to read more, to expand my horizons, so to speak.

With the reading finished, I spent the final day on the trail cogitating about Diana Kilkenny and the threatening note I'd received. Was it simply the expression from a woman who felt scorned, or was there an interested rival who wanted me out of the picture?

The man's steed drank deeply from the meandering waters of the Guadalupe. He'd ridden hard to arrive at the appointed time. He was a tall slender figure of a man and wore a cowboy's chaps and broad-brimmed hat. Looking to be all business, he pulled a gold-encased pocket watch from his vest and checked the time. He patted the withers of the well-lathered horse. He grew agitated, as though annoyed that someone would be late. Scanning his surroundings, he couldn't hear the hammer pulled back above the sounds of the river at night. Moonlight reflected from the waters and cast him as a silhouette against the starlit sky.

With his back to the river, he couldn't see the flash from the rifle muzzle. The bullet entering his back was surely felt. The rifle's explosive report would have been heard had it not been too late. His hand went to the gaping hole in his chest. He gazed with shock at his bloodied hand, then placed it against the horse to steady himself. He left a smear of blood as he dropped to his knees and fell face forward onto the bank of the Guadalupe River. He convulsed and tried to rise, as his inert form slid into the warm waters of the river.

A shadowy figure on the opposite shore grinned at the successful kill, mounted up, and rode into the night, leaving behind further mystery to shroud the Guadalupe.

Sheriff Vann shook his head in dismay. It had been only two days since the Texas Ranger sent to help him had left for Nuecestown, and now he had another murder on his hands. He was no closer to a solution.

Of course, I couldn't have known, and another murder at this point—while lamentable—wasn't preventable. I had yet to have been much help in solving the series of murders that shook the citizens of Kerrville to their very bones.

NINE
HOME

THE GATEWAY ARCH to Heaven's Gate Ranch loomed ahead. It was great to be home, as I realized how much I'd missed Cassie these past few weeks. I reckoned I just might get over to visit my dad and get his advice on the mess in Kerrville, but first things first.

I patted Tornado's neck and cantered up the lane. Understand that I love my horse, but he played second fiddle by a long shot to Cassie. I reined in at the house, slipped from my saddle, and bounded up the front steps. Before I could grab the latch, the door swung open, and Cassie was in my arms. My, but she felt incredibly good. I responded accordingly.

Cassie drew back and looked down at the bulge in my pants. A wanton smile parted her lips. Lust overcame us. With nary a word, she pulled me inside, pushed me down, opened my drawers, and was satisfying our carnal desires. Weeks without each other fed our passions.

We lay on the foyer carpet, basking in the afterglow. Cassie's head lay on my chest.

"I missed you, Mr. Texas Ranger," she cooed.

I was about to respond, when a plaintive cry broke the stillness of the moment and brought us out of our pleasure-fed moment. Sean had awakened and likely needed feeding. It was a stark reminder of the responsibilities I shouldered and reinforced my having rejected the lustful advances of Diana Kilkenny.

Cassie buttoned her dress as she arose to see to our young son.

I pulled myself together, grabbed some sugar, and headed back outside to see to Tornado. I led him to the stable, where he received a well-deserved currying and sugar cube treats. I saw a mare a couple of stalls away grab his attention. It struck me how similar male desires could be, regardless of species. "Later, big fellow," I assured him. He stomped his feet with impatient reply.

By the time I was back in our kitchen, Cassie had fed Sean and was brewing some coffee. "Set yourself, and tell me how it went."

"Well, the case hasn't been solved. There were four murders, and while there's circumstantial evidence and plenty of motivations, there's not enough hard evidence to pin the killings on anyone. I reckon to visit Dad and pluck his brain. He might think of something I've missed." I sipped some coffee. Dang, but Cassie sure brewed great coffee.

"Any suspects?" she asked.

"Something isn't all square about the daughter of a Galveston businessman who bought a ranch close to Kerrville. I haven't quite figured it out, though the whole town's abuzz over her flirtatious ways," I replied. "And wouldn't you know, but Archer Parr may be involved somehow."

"Did she tempt you?" pressed Cassie.

"She tried," I reckoned it best to be honest. "But no, I wasn't tempted." I dared not admit how difficult it had been to fend off Diana Kilkenny's wiles. "Her father lent me a couple of books. He seems honest enough, but he may be involved."

"So, you spent some time with them?"

"Only what was necessary to figure whether they had any connection to the murders. Land appears to be the motivation for the killings, as the victims thus far had no heirs to their properties." I didn't want to dwell on Diana Kilkenny. "I also reckon to give a visit to Archer Parr while I'm here."

Cassie smiled at her fears of me being tempted to infidelity. She sidled over to me and placed my hand on her belly. "We're going to bring another Dunn into the world, Lucas." She gave me a sweet hug and a kiss. "I'll have dinner ready in a couple of hours," she said over her shoulder while ambling over to the stove. "Why don't you reacquaint yourself with Heaven's Gate."

I swallowed the last drop from my cup as I arose, walked over behind her, and wrapped my arms around her. "I've missed you, Cassie McCully Dunn." With that, I headed out to refamiliarize myself with our ranch. Mother and Dad had ceded Heaven's Gate proper to the land Mr. McCully had given us as a wedding gift, so our holdings had become quite substantial.

I headed to the graves up on the hill near the ranch house. My mother's parents and siblings were buried there along with my brother after having been killed in a Comanche attack on the homestead. The .45 casings were still nestled among the grasses and flowers atop my brother's grave, where my mother had strewn them after killing his murderer. A way off were the graves of a pair of

Comanche warriors killed by my mother and father in a subsequent attack. Those were surely tough times. I chuckled at the thought of them being first-generation Irish immigrants and mixing an Irish lilt with Texas twang in their voices. They'd endured in love and life. It'd be good to pay a visit.

I let Tornado loose in the corral with the mare he'd cast his eyes upon. I'm sure he was grateful, as to the mare—only time would tell.

I checked out the bunkhouse. We had two cowboys helping, but they were off likely chasing down strays.

By the time I was done with my musings and explorations, dinner hour had approached. Cassie set a wonderful table filled with the bounty of a better-than-usual ranching year. I'd rigged a contraption for baby Sean that fitted to a chair such that he could see us at mealtime.

"When shall we visit your folks, Lucas?" asked Cassie.

"Well, they're right close by, but I'm of a mind to visit Archer Parr first. It might bring me some additional perspective as to the goings on in Kerrville."

Cassie looked at this as her husband being away for another couple of days.

I caught the disappointed look in her eyes. "What say we picnic tomorrow? We can mosey to that spot we love along the Nueces River."

"I'd like that, Lucas," she replied with a loving smile. "I'd like that a lot."

I sensed that an evening of dessert lay ahead, and we wouldn't be getting much sleep.

I had been up early to muck stalls and a few other chores before we left for our picnic. I had Tornado saddled along

with Cassie's mare—not the one my trusty Appaloosa stallion had mated with. My 1895 Winchester was nestled in its
saddle scabbard, and I carried a brand-new Smith &
Wesson revolver. One couldn't be too careful. I led the
horses to the ranch house and hitched them out front. I was
about to head inside, when Cassie appeared at the front
door carrying Sean and a picnic basket.

My mouth dropped. Diana Kilkenny could learn a few
things on true sexiness. Cassie's dress, cut low across her
chest and form-fitting from the waist up, was arousing to
say the least. Even the still very slight bump of her child-
laden belly held a certain provocativeness.

"Are you going to just stand there, Lucas Dunn?" she
chided with a smile.

I relieved her of her bundles and watched appreciatively
as she climbed into the mare's saddle. I handed Sean to her,
then mounted, hooked the basket on my saddle and
mounted up. The Nueces was only a couple of miles away,
and the landscape was mostly flat and covered with grasses
sprinkled with mesquite, a few cacti, and occasional live
oak. Our property abutted the river, so we were assured of
some level of privacy. Even the couple of hands that helped
us with the ranch knew to stay away when the boss lady
and her husband sought private time.

Our chosen spot was a pecan tree along the riverbank.
In fact, the pecan tree's fruit was the river's namesake. I
helped Sean and Cassie down from her saddle, and we
spread a blanket for our picnic.

I laid out the goodies Cassie had packed while she
nursed Sean until he fell asleep. I popped the cork on the
wine bottle and filled two crystal goblets with our home-
made vino. We enjoyed smoked venison and cheese then
lay back to enjoy the sky above and the beauty surrounding
us. Cassie nuzzled my shoulder, then began unbuttoning

my shirt and slowly stroking my chest. It wasn't long before more than my shirt had been opened to her probing fingers.

Cassie hiked up her skirt and mounted my hips while unbuttoning her bodice. My hands explored her swollen breasts as she took me within her. We were utterly consuming ourselves with passion, when a rifle blast exploded from the far shore of the Nueces, and a bullet whizzed past Cassie's head and into the pecan tree above us. I rolled us both over behind the tree. This was not the climax to our tryst that we'd been seeking.

I peeked from around the tree trunk in time to see someone riding off at full gallop in a cloud of prairie dust. I could only see the back of the rider. Whoever it was wore a black hat and jacket and rode a black cayuse. Was the intention to kill us or scare us? How did the shooter know where we'd be? Why and Who?

Well, it sure took the edge from our picnic. Cassie was shaking like aspen leaves in a high wind. "Lucas...Lucas, are we okay?"

Sean began to cry. Thankfully, he'd been unhurt. As Cassie sought to soothe our baby son, I handed her my revolver, mounted Tornado, and plunged into the river. I was determined to find any evidence the shooter may have left behind.

This was a time when I was grateful that my horse was strong, the river was low, and the current was weak. I made it to the opposite shore and dismounted at roughly the area from where I figured the shooter had fired his shot. The dirt kicked up by his horse's hooves made it easier. In but a minute of looking around, the reflection of sunlight on nickel, led me to a cartridge case. The shooter was either sloppy or purposely left this clue. The shooter had used an Army-issue rifle, likely a Springfield 1892 with a .30-40 cartridge. Like the 1895 Winchesters I'd faced in pursuing the vigilante, this rifle was common enough to make finding the perpetrator unlikely. The shooter left a few boot imprints, but there seemed nothing special. I continued examining the scene while keeping an eye on Cassie and Shawn across the river. I was about to give up on finding anything significant, when a piece of blue silk ribbon caught my eye. Its ragged edges suggested that it had been torn from something. I stuffed it in my pocket, made a final scan of the area, and headed back to Cassie.

"Find anything?" asked Cassie.

"Cartridge case and a piece of blue ribbon. Not much to go on," I replied. "Are you ready to head home?"

Cassie gave me a look as though pondering my question. "Is the shooter gone?"

I responded with a curious expression. What was she suggesting?

"Sean is asleep," she whispered and opened her bodice to me.

I didn't have to be asked twice. Shucks, whoever had shot at us was long gone.

I sat on the gallery the next morning, sipping coffee and thinking on yesterday's picnic adventure.

Cassie came out and sat beside me. "So who is this Archer Parr and how do you think he's involved with the Kerrville killings?"

I was pleased that she was earnestly interested. "Archie is sort of an enigma. His father fought with Zachary Taylor in the Mexican War back in 1846 and fathered five children. From what I've been told, Archie was an industrious lad from an early age. He wrangled horses, drove cattle, and was even a trail boss on a Chisholm Trail drive before he turned eighteen. He taught school a bit, then headed to Duval County where he managed The Sweden Ranch and then bought his own spread. He married and began raising a family, but ranching success wasn't enough. Given that Mexicans constituted the majority of residents, he befriended enough of them to get himself elected as a county commissioner. That's sort of where his life journey stands today. As a rancher and politician, he has a habit of making interesting liaisons with all manner of influential folks. While nothing appears outwardly shady, there are suspicions floating about. You know how rumors can take on a life of their own."

"Why do you think he's tied into the Kerrville matter?"

"Not sure that he is. But Parr seeks to be an influencer. To do that, he must build personal wealth and the connections leading to wealth and power. Power is often a dangerous elixir."

"Elixir?" asked Cassie.

"It's a powerful concoction that muddles straight thinking much as liquor does."

"And you think he might be involved?"

"Well, I'm not fixing to come right out and accuse him of anything. I just want him to know that he's on my mind."

"San Diego and back is a day's ride. Shall I invite your folks over the day after tomorrow?"

"I'm suspecting you're of a mind to feed 'em big," I said with a chuckle.

"I finally figured out the special ingredient in those mesquite logs your mother cooked with."

"Ha! You really figured it out?" I said with a laugh. I was one of the few that kept the family secret and doubted that Cassie really knew.

"I'm sure of it."

"What is it then?" I asked with a devious smile.

"It's something not mentionable in polite company," she said confidently.

"She has figured it out," I said to myself. "Well, who knows? You just might be on to something," I teased. "Speaking of which, I need to tend to nature out back."

Cassie hit me playfully with a dish towel.

I headed out the back door toward the outhouse, laughing all the way. I stopped at the woodpile with its separate stack of mesquite branches and looked back to be sure Cassie wasn't looking before adding the special ingredient.

San Diego was a sleepy little town abutting Alice, the namesake of Richard King's daughter. The county seat of Duval County, San Diego, was a ranching town that survived in part from the economic largesse of the railroad hub around which Alice had been built.

It was just before Noon when I made my way through the gate at Archie Parr's ranch and headed to his house. There was nothing special about the spread. A few head of beeves grazed here and there. They looked to be Herefords.

There was nothing humble about Archie Parr's home. It was no mansion, mind you, but it was well-kept and quite well-appointed. I had to remind myself that, despite his dabbling in the mostly ungentlemanly realm of politics, he was an experienced ranch hand. He knew what it took to run a successful spread.

A household servant parked me in a cozy room that apparently served as Parr's office and library. He possessed an impressive book collection not unlike Kilkenny. I got to admire the beautiful wood-paneled walls and the modest-sized but ornately-carved mahogany desk. Parr was late. It was a habit I came to find in those who sought to exercise power and manipulate others.

The door finally opened, and a smiling Archie Parr strode in with hand outstretched. "Texas Ranger Dunn! What an honor to make your acquaintance," he announced.

"Thank you, sir. I appreciate you seeing me on such short notice."

"I heard about you from Sheriff Forto and my friend Steve Powers. Seems you've been hard at work lifting the already fine reputation of the Texas Rangers."

I was surprised that a certain foul odor hadn't begun to reach my nose. Parr was already piling on the compliments. "Why, thank you," I responded.

"I'm sure Captain Hughes appreciates you, Ranger Dunn." He opened a humidor on his desk and offered me a cigar. Upon shaking my head, he pulled one out, nipped one end, and lit it up. "So, what brings you all the way to San Diego?"

I reckoned to be straightforward, especially as I was seeking to observe his reaction to what I had to say. "Well, I'm investigating a series of murders on the Guadalupe River up in Kerrville. I chatted with Joseph Kilkenny, and he mentioned his being acquainted with you." I observed Parr stiffen just a tad. "Since I'd already heard about you from Sheriff Forto down in Brownsville, I figured time was due for us to meet."

"I hear that Joseph is doing quite well in Kerrville," noted Parr. "That daughter of his sure is a pistol," he added.

I nodded and smiled. "I got the impression that Mr. Kilkenny was interested in expanding his ranch holdings." I strove to ignore the comment about Diana. For all I knew, Parr might have even enjoyed a dalliance with her.

"Dunn? Are you associated with that famous Texas

Ranger Luke Dunn?" It was a clumsy attempt to change the subject.

I nodded.

"So, you've come all the way from Kerrville just to meet me? I'm honored."

"I had some responsibilities to tend to at home, so I reckoned it was high time we got acquainted. I can't stay long, as my wife has plans that need my attention." I sat back and took a long gander at Parr, as he sent cigar smoke skyward in small circles. "I don't suppose you have any interest in properties around Kerrville?" I ventured.

Parr never missed a beat. "Shucks, Ranger, I've got plenty to handle around these parts." He gave me a wry smile. "And I don't have to have blood on my hands."

Parr was no dummy. He knew full well why I was there. "I would never think to accuse anyone of your standing of such foul actions, Mr. Parr."

"You can call me Archie," he said with a forced smile.

"Well, I do appreciate your time, Archie. Perhaps, we can enjoy a longer meeting in the future." I arose from my seat. "I see that you enjoy literary arts," I said, motioning to the bookcases. "There's a lot to be learned from books. Kilkenny lent me a couple."

Parr snuffed out his cigar and escorted me to the door. "It's good to know that our law enforcement men are seeking to improve themselves with book learning. It's been a pleasure meeting you, Texas Ranger Dunn." He motioned toward the front door. I took the silent invitation and departed.

As I rode up the trail to the ranch entrance, I sensed that I was being watched. I didn't feel threatened, but stayed alert nevertheless.

I wasn't sure I'd accomplished a whole lot during my brief meeting with Parr. If nothing else, it placed him on notice that I was working the murders in Kerrville. I'd found his reaction interesting but hardly conclusive toward any involvement. Kerrville was a goodly distance away from San Diego, but politics tended to expand politician's reach. In any case, he'd been right quick to assure me that he wasn't involved.

I looked forward to asking my dad what he thought of Archie Parr. He'd surely have an honest point of view. I gave Tornado extra heels to his flanks, and we trotted a while. I breathed deeply and let the clear air fill my lungs. I was anxious to get home.

The return ride from San Diego was decidedly uneventful. While fears of Indian attacks had pretty much found their way to the history books, there was always the danger of bandits, most often of Mexican descent and often aspiring to be the next rebel leader. Riding alone demanded a wariness born of experience in these things. My being well-armed would tend to discourage any bandit who thought twice about giving me any trouble.

The long ride did give me time to think on the previous day's picnic. I was pretty certain that whoever had taken a shot at me had missed intentionally. The casing and ribbon fragment just might have been left behind on purpose. Diana's flirtatiousness, the threatening note, and then a suspicious ambush combined to gather that someone was trying to discourage my pursuit of the Kerrville killer. On the other hand, was someone who knew who the killer was, leaving me clues?

It felt great to finally ride through the Heaven's Gate gateway arch and up the trail toward home.

Walking into the foyer of our home, now referred to as

the "big house" by virtue of its standing as the ranch head-quarters dwelling, I took in the aromas wafting from the kitchen. It smelled as though Cassie sure had been busy.

As I closed the door, I caught sight of my folks approaching. I expected to see them driving the wagon, but they'd chosen to ride horses. I suppose it made some sense, given that they lived a mere five miles away. My dad was riding a big black stallion, while mom looked beautiful aboard a gray mare. With all of my dad's aches and pains earned from better than twenty years of delivering justice as a Texas Ranger on the Nueces Strip and now nearly sixty years old, I found myself impressed with his horsemanship. The two of them looked right fine.

"Cassie, I'm home!" I called. "My folks are in sight."

She appeared in the kitchen doorway in a figure-flat-tering blue gingham dress. Her belly bump was barely noticeable. I strode over and wiped a bit of flour from her chin, as I delivered a kiss. "We're just about ready, Lucas. Get yourself cleaned up." She smiled demurely and turned back to the kitchen.

About the time I was toweling off from the washbasin, my folks were knocking on the front door. "I've got it!" I called to Cassie.

I opened the door to a right handsome-looking couple. I only hoped that Cassie and I might age as well as my folks. "Welcome," I intoned as I hugged each and escorted them to the parlor beside the dining room. Of course, they needed no direction, as they'd raised ten children in this home.

Cassie poked her head in. "We'll be dining in a moment," she said invitingly and blew a kiss.

★★

Well, Cassie served up a delectable feast to be remembered. She winked at me, as I sliced the roast brisket. She was convinced that she'd figured out the secret ingredient in the mesquite firewood. I didn't even flinch when my dad complimented her on the flavor.

After dinner, we gathered in the parlor. I served up some wine made from grapes grown in our own orchard and reckoned it was time to broach the questions that had been dogging me the past couple of weeks.

"What do you think of Archer Parr, Dad?" I said after enjoying a sip of wine.

Luke Dunn licked his own lips. "Delicious," he noted. "I mean the wine, not Archie Parr," he said with a smile.

Cassie and my mom smiled graciously at Dad's humor.

"Parr is an up-and-comer, Junior. There's an old adage about keeping your friends close and enemies closer. I'd say that Archie Parr is somewhere between those two conditions. He's honest to a point, but watch your backtrail. He's an ambitious man."

I nodded that I understood. "Captain Hughes assigned me to help Sheriff Vann up in Kerrville with a series of murders that coincidentally have all occurred at night on the banks of the Guadalupe River. Three of the killings seem to have involved the killer cleaning up witnesses. The common connection of two of the victims has been land with no heirs. Their ranches happen to adjoin the ranch of a successful shipping magnate from Galveston and new ranch owner named Joseph Kilkenny. I've chatted with Kilkenny, and he seems honest enough. He also seems to be loosely associated with Archer Parr. There's some physical evidence surrounding the murders, but not enough to pin the killings on anyone." I paused, watching my dad stroke his mustache as was his habit when deep in thought. "Kilkenny's daughter is quite flirtatious and has a less-than-stellar reputation from the gossip around Kerrville. Since visiting Kilkenny, I've received a threatening note and been shot at, though I think the shooter missed deliberately. He left behind a bullet casing and a fragment of blue ribbon. What do you think?"

My dad, retired legendary Texas Ranger Luke Dunn, cleared his throat. "That's a humdinger of a tale, son," he uttered with his thick Irish accent mixed with Texas drawl. "I've heard of this fellow up in northeastern Texas and Oklahoma neat Fort Smith named Bass Reeves. He's a deputy US Marshal and is building a reputation for tracking down and capturing lawbreakers." Dad stroked his mustache a bit more. "Reeves is about your size. Happens to be a Black man, an escaped slave. Funny thing is that he's illiterate—can't read a lick. Has somebody read the warrants to him and memorizes them. Anyhow, he might be of some help."

"What would you do?" I persisted.

"I'd get some advice for a situation like this. Go meet Bass Reeves," he insisted. "Alternatively, you can keep digging, but it could get you killed from the sound of it." He glanced at Cassie. "In my experience, I sought to shy away from that sort of outcome," he said with a knowing chuckle. He stroked his mustache and turned serious. "Today's world of bringing folks to justice is the same but different. The moral characteristics of bad people haven't changed much though their methods of lawbreaking can be more complex. You've got better communications and weapons today, but guns aren't always the answer and a telephone won't corral a killer. You must still outthink the bad guys. Oh, and I'd add greater patience and cunning to the skill set a good lawman must bring to his profession."

I took a long sip of wine.

Cassie smiled. From her late grandfather to her father-in-law to her husband, her life was inexorably linked to men dedicated to bringing justice to the land. She held a mix of pride and fear for my safety. "Lucas will solve the case," she said confidently.

"Well, I think he might just do that," said my dad reassuringly.

My mom looked over at Cassie, and her eyes fell to my loving wife's midsection. "Is there something you're not telling us?" My, but she sure had an active intuition.

"Sean's going to have a brother or sister," said a blushing Cassie.

"Well, I'll be doggoned!" exclaimed my dad. "Congratulations to you both."

It was getting late, and the evening was wearing on my aging parents. They'd have a right nice ride ahead under starry moonlit skies. It had been a wonderful evening, but I knew that I'd have to bring my attentions back to the Kerrville matter. I had not yet heard that there'd been another killing.

"Are you going to seek out this Bass Reeves fellow?" asked Cassie, as we enjoyed breakfast.

"Reckon I should heed my dad's advice. No point in asking for it, if I don't take it."

"It's a long ride to Fort Smith," she observed.

"Maybe I should look into traveling by train, though Tornado might be jealous," I said with a chortle.

"Didn't Mr. Kilkenny give you two books?" Cassie was suggesting that I could read *Huckleberry Finn* while riding Tornado to northeastern Texas.

I was looking at nearly three weeks by horseback and no more than two days by train. I could find a temporary saddle nag up around the fort. After seeing Reeves, I could return to Nuecestown and ride Tornado to Kerrville. "I think the train makes sense," I said decisively. "I'd better send a message to Sheriff Vann, so he knows what I'm up to."

TEN
SEEKING HELP

MIND YOU, I'm major proud of my dad's legendary accomplishments as a lawman, but I must admit from all I'd heard, that this Bass Reeves fellow he advised me to seek out was one of the very best ever. It didn't take much digging to learn that Reeves spoke several Indian languages and was famed as a gunfighter and scout. Like my dad told me, Reeves was a runaway slave. As I understood it, Reeves dealt with a host of lawbreakers, including bandits, rustlers, horse thieves, murderers, and more. Like me, his choice of weapons leaned to Winchester rifles and Colt revolvers. It especially impressed me that he had tracked down and killed the notorious outlaw, Jim Webb, in a shootout. Webb had been credited with murdering more than eleven people. Desperadoes, no matter whether White, Black, or Indian, wound up arrested or shot and killed by Bass Reeves.

The journey to Fort Smith up on the Arkansas River in the state of that name would necessarily be complicated, as there was no direct rail line from Corpus Christi. I had a few transfers ahead of me. The upside was it being far faster travel than horseback.

I fired off a telegram to Sheriff Vann, informing him of my intentions and that I expected to return to Kerrville as quickly as possible. I held back any reference to the apparently faked bushwhacking. There was a part of me that hoped the killer would be found during my absence.

As I was about to leave the telegraph office, the proprietor, Hap Carlson, hailed me. "Hang on a Texas second, Junior. This came in last night." He waved a telegram at me. "It's from that Vann fella yuh jus' sent the telegram to."

A quick read revealed news of a fifth murder on the Guadalupe. Vann must have been none too pleased that I was absent from Kerrville. "Dang, Hap. I'd better send another message." I reckoned that I'd better acknowledge receipt of Vann's message. It wouldn't change my plans, but a reply was simply the proper thing to do.

Turned out that Hap handled tickets for the train, so he mapped out my route with the various transfers. As it worked out, I'd be leaving the next morning.

Business in Corpus completed, I headed back to Heaven's Gate. I reckoned to make the most of the night with Cassie. I expect Tornado must have sensed something was up, because he headed us home at a fast walk without my urging.

It was a crystal-clear day, and I had yet to encounter any travelers on the road from Corpus. Yet, I had a sense that I had company. As much as I was anxious to get home, I found myself listening to my intuitive sense. Perhaps, the bushwhacking incident made me overly sensitive. I made a turn toward Nueces Bay, then back-trailed about a half mile. Nothing. No sign, no sound. If someone was tailing me, they were especially good at staying hidden. I shook my head resignedly and returned to the road. Maybe I was just being a tad gun-shy.

Cassie was waiting on the gallery nursing Sean when I reined in. I dismounted, bounded up the stairs, and enjoyed a bounty of kisses and hugs.

"Take care of Tornado then hustle in for dinner," said Cassie with a demure smile. "You can tell me about Corpus and your plans."

I led Tornado off to the stable. Just as I entered the barn, I caught movement in my peripheral vision. I stopped and looked in that direction. There was no sign. I turned and looked over at the nearby bunkhouse, and our hands were busy with personal chores. I looked back from where I could swear that I saw someone or something, but there was nothing. I led Tornado into his stall and unsaddled and curried him. The situation sure had my hackles up.

Tornado cared for, I washed up and headed for the big house and what would surely be a wonderful dinner. There seemed no point in mentioning my suspicions to Cassie.

"So, you're following your dad's advice."

"Yep. Bought the tickets and have my transfers laid out. Figure to leave tomorrow morning and be at Fort Smith in about two days." I stuffed a forkful of potatoes into my mouth.

"Did you let Sheriff Vann know?" she asked.

"Yep. Got a telegram off to him." I responded a little mechanically.

"What else?" she probed.

I sighed. "Been another killing on the Guadalupe up in Kerrville," I replied matter-of-factly.

"I'll bet the sheriff is none too happy about that."

"Well, I've got to do what I've got to do. My dad thinks this Reeves fellow might give me some good advice."

Cassie sighed, one of those whatever-will-be will-be sighs.

"I'll try not to be too long at Fort Smith. I did telegraph an inquiry to Judge Parker, and he fully expects Reeves to be there. Assuming the trains run on time, I'll arrive on July 29." I mouthed another forkful from my plate. "I don't expect to be spending more than a couple of days at Fort Smith. I hope to be back here in a few days, then I'll have to turn around and head back to Kerrville." I paused thought-fully. "Maybe, I'll take a train to Kerrville and bring Tornado in the car with the livestock if one's available. I do like the faster travel."

Cassie nodded. "You do have it all planned. I'm impressed, Mr. Texas Ranger,"

Dinner, topped with peach pie for dessert, was finished. We exchanged knowing looks.

"Go put Sean to bed. I'll clean up." I likely wouldn't match her cleanliness standard, but I'd get the kitchen in order right quick.

She smiled and ambled off to the nursery.

I wasted no time. I was about to head to our bedroom when I felt compelled to look out the front window. Dark-ness had descended, but the shadowy form of a rider moved across the front yard. It wasn't one of our hands, as lights were on in the bunkhouse, and I could make both of them out. It didn't take a mental giant to figure that whoever was riding through was likely up to something nefarious. There was nothing I could do this night in the dark. That would be a fool's game.

Cassie appeared at the door to our bedroom. "Everything all right?" she asked.

I turned disconcertedly. She stood fetchingly with a diaphanous nothing wrapped around her shoulders. "Er, yes. Everything's fine." I tried not to show the concern surely written across my face as I strode over and took her in my arms. "Dang, but you sure look sexy," I said as I laid her on our bed. Her wrap fell away, my pants dropped, and she was all mine. Boots and shirt would have to wait.

Turned out there was no space for Tornado, so I stabled him at a cousin's smithy shop in Corpus Christi and headed to the train station. I had timed my departure from Heaven's Gate perfectly, though it had been very difficult to muster the energy to depart after such a night of unbridled carnality. Cassie made certain I'd not be forgetting her womanly charms. Plus, she sent me off with a bag of fresh-baked bear sign. We still hadn't shifted to calling those goodies donuts.

I still sensed that I was being followed, but had yet to identify my pursuer. There had been no overt threat as yet. That got me to thinking that whoever was tailing me might be spying on my movements. Now, there was something I hadn't considered. A spy. Could it be my fake bushwhacker? Who might be employing him? Why was it necessary to trace my movements? I resolved to be extra-sensitive to my surroundings on the chance my pursuer might inadvertently reveal himself.

I leaned against the train station's front wall, keeping my eyes peeled as folks moved back and forth on the station platform. I was traveling light with only my saddlebags and the clothes on my back. My Smith & Wesson revolver was strapped down in the holster on my hip, and my Bowie knife was sheathed on the opposite hip. There had seemed no need to bring much of an arsenal. I made sure that my Texas Ranger badge was plainly visible on my shirt to reassure fellow passengers that I was no roving troublemaker with a gun for hire.

The train chugged into the station with squealing wheels and bursts of steam. I observed about a dozen people climb aboard before I boarded the coach and found a seat beside a window. I reckoned to take in the Texas scenery. I wondered whether my shadowy pursuer was on the train with me? With these closer quarters, he just might accidentally reveal himself. I casually looked around at my fellow passengers. No one stood out as being worthy of consideration as a spy. There I was tossed in with a bunch of strangers headed to who knows where. Had I not seen that shadowy rider in the darkness as Heaven's Gate the night before, I might have chalked the entire spy business up to a very active imagination.

I had picked up a newspaper at the station, so I opened it up and began reading. From time to time, I looked up to gaze out the window and then scan the passengers to see whether anyone seemed to have a special interest in me. If someone was spying on me, they were right good at their craft. I reckoned it would be interesting to see which passengers shared my itinerary. I had four train transfers ahead so I reckoned that would afford plenty of opportunity.

My luck as to schedules and timing was holding up quite well. The train pulled into Houston on schedule, enabling me to take the Gulf Line to Palestine. I planned to spend the night there, then be boarding another train heading to Longview, Marshall, and finally on to Fort Smith. If my fortunes held up, I'd arrive at Fort Smith on July 29 as scheduled.

Most of the passengers transferred in Houston, and once again, no one stood out as following me. Perhaps, I was seeing things after all.

I turned my attention back to the newspaper. There was an article about a rising star politician named Theodore Roosevelt, who was the police commissioner of New York City but had higher aspirations. The writer of the article stressed Roosevelt's toughness as a rancher and outdoorsman. I admired the photograph of the man shown in his buckskins and hunting rifle. A severe winter hit North Dakota in 1887 and caused his ranch to fail, so he headed back east and immersed himself in public service. From the tenor of the article, it appeared he was indeed headed for great accomplishments. Admittedly, it got me to thinking whether politics might be in my very own future.

I folded the newspaper and was about to shut my eyes when a passenger walked past me toward the back of the coach. He had avoided looking at me. I turned and watched him exit the door to an observation deck. I could swear that I saw him pull something from a pocket and toss it out. I quickly turned back, as he re-entered the coach and strode past me to his seat. He sat with his back to me, so I had yet to make out his facial features. He wasn't a big man, but there was a certain stealthiness about the way he walked. A black broad-brimmed hat shaded half his face from view, and he wore a black jacket that seemed a bit heavy for the Texas heat. He wore a gun hung in a holster worn low on his right hip.

The train pulled into Longview, and my eyes scanned the passengers. Naturally, I kept an especially wary eye on the traveler with the black hat. The number of passengers from the initial boarding back in Corpus had dissipated to a mere handful. The wiry fellow in that black hat was among them. I noted that he seemed to go out of his way to avoid any eye contact with me. That sure seemed telling and fed my suspicions.

By the time we transferred at Marshall to the line north to Fort Smith, there were only three of us from the original folks who'd boarded back in Corpus. I did note that the black-hatted traveler spent an inordinate time with the telegraph operator at the Marshall train station. The third traveler was a nondescript sort that I wouldn't suspect of anything nefarious. A slightly-built fellow in a vested gray suit, he looked every bit like a city-slicker. He carried a black leather case, which led me to think he was some sort of salesman.

As the train drew close to Fort Smith, I turned my thoughts to meeting this Bass Reeves lawman that my father had recommended. In reaching out to Judge Parker's folks, I learned that Reeves would be at Fort Smith to witness a hanging. Reeves had apparently helped bring a swindler, thief, and forger named Wilson to justice over a murder. Wilson's real name was James Casharego. Apparently, Wilson had an erstwhile partner named Zachariah Thatch. Wilson imbibed heavily one night at the Red Dog Saloon in Keokuk Falls, Oklahoma. In whatever melee ensued afterward, Wilson used an axe and gun to murder Thatch and tried to hide the body among rocks and tree branches beside Rock Creek near the North Canadian River. Reeves and another deputy named Eddie Reed arrested Wilson a few days later up on the Kickapoo Reservation. Wilson claimed innocence, but confessed when Reeves and Reed confronted him with Thatch's corpse and the axe in Wilson's wagon. Reeves even found the campsite where the murder had occurred and the spot where Wilson had built a fire over the bloody soil where his victim had bled out. Reeves dug beneath the ashes and found soil soaked with Thatch's blood. Reeves subsequently testified at Wilson's trial, and Judge Parker sentenced the man to death by hanging. The execution of James Casharego was scheduled for July 30, 1896. I reckoned that Reeves witnessing the event would afford me the opportunity to meet the famed lawman. I hoped and prayed that he'd find time for me.

I stepped gingerly from the St Louis and San Francisco Railroad train onto the platform at the Fort Smith station. It was a bustling hub of activity. I naturally glanced around at my surroundings. The fellow in the gray suit continued on the train, but my black-hatted companion disembarked and disappeared up the platform with nary a look back at me. Maybe, my imagination had simply been overly active.

I inquired as to directions to the nearest hotel. There was plenty of time to locate the site of the hanging and wrangle a meeting with Reeves. It turned out that the Lindell Hotel was just up the street from the train depot. The hotel had a fresh new-construction aroma about it. I approached the lobby desk and was greeted by a friendly young man.

"I'm interested in a room for a couple of nights," I said.

The young man spun a registry book around to me. His eyes gave me a once-over as though judging my character. "Sure enough, sir. Just sign in here. We do request payment in advance," he advised with an expression just shy of condescending.

I signed in and was handed a key to a room with a view of the Arkansas River.

"Texas Ranger, eh?" noted the desk clerk. "Guess you're out of your jurisdiction here in Arkansas," he said with a satisfied-looking half smile.

"Where may a hungry Texas Ranger find good victuals around here?" I inquired.

"We serve dinner here after six o'clock," he responded with a finger to a clock on the wall. It was half-past six. He gave me another once-over, along with a sleazy sort of facial expression. If you have any interest in dessert, there are a few fine establishments that might answer any pleasures you might have in mind." The way he provocatively drew out the word "dessert" left nothing to the imagination. Apparently, the neighborhood abounded with soiled doves anxious to service visitors.

"I'm just here to witness tomorrow's hanging," I said with obvious disinterest in the young man's dessert suggestion. With that, I tipped my hat and headed to the dining room.

The desk clerk gave me a decidedly disappointed look.

My introduction to Fort Smith was enlightening as to some folks' natures. I was determined to enjoy a good meal and have a restful night's sleep.

The gallows at Fort Smith were a rather fancy affair. The structure could handle as many as a half dozen executions simultaneously. The talkative desk clerk at the Lindell Hotel had given me directions and added that nearly ninety executions had been performed at the Fort Smith gallows. It was little wonder that they called Judge Parker the "hanging judge." The desk clerk lamented that this Casharego felon was to be the last man to hang at these gallows.

A crowd had gathered for the event, likely as much to experience a perverted sort of thinking that enjoys seeing a human being hung by the neck until death as to be witnesses to this final hanging. I scanned the gathering and soon made out a tall, stern-looking Black man sporting a great mustache. He fit the description of Bass Reeves that I'd been given. He looked to be all business.

I was now faced with introducing myself. I'd already garnered some attention by virtue of my Texas Ranger badge being on full display. I was about to head toward Reeves when a hand grasped my arm. I found myself staring into the mustachioed face of a well-dressed man.

"Are you the Texas Ranger that inquired about Deputy Marshal Reeves?" came the inquiry.

I nodded distractedly.

"I'm Judge Isaac Parker. I've heard about your father and have looked forward to meeting you," he stated with enthusiasm.

"Why, thank you, sir. It's a pleasure to make your acquaintance," I responded. We shook hands.

"What's your business with Marshal Reeves?"

"I'm handling a difficult multiple-murder case back in Kerrville, and my father suggested that Marshal Reeves might have some advice."

"Your father is a very wise man," assured Parker. "Bass Reeves will surely go down in history as one of the best US Deputy Marshals ever."

"I'm looking forward to meeting him, judge," I stated, with hope of getting an introduction to Reeves.

"Well, let's observe the proceedings, and then I'll be pleased to formally introduce you."

We turned simultaneously at a gasp from the crowd. A noose had been placed around the neck of the hooded felon on the gallows. So far as I could tell, Casharego had no final words.

There was an eerie silence. It was so quiet that I could swear I heard sobbing from the man who was about to meet his fate.

Judge Parker gave a nearly imperceptible nod. A door

fell open beneath Casharego, and he instantly dropped so far as the noose would allow. There was a snapping sound. Casharego twitched once and hung limp. A hush of approval arose from the onlookers.

"Come on, Dunn. I'll introduce you to Marshal Reeves," offered Parker in his next breath.

I followed him through the dispersing crowd, my eyes riveted on the tall Black man we headed toward. Everyone stepped back in deference to Judge Parker.

Reeves had turned to head toward the stable. With his duty done, it seemed he was fixing to depart. He was apparently a humble man and all business so far as his duties were concerned.

"Marshal!" called out Parker.

Reeves paused mid-stride and turned to meet Parker. "Yes sir, your honor," responded Reeves quite respectfully.

"I have a fellow I'd like you to meet."

Reeves gave me an appraising look. His eyes dropped from my face to the Texas Ranger badge on my shirt, as it shined brightly in the mid-morning sunshine. He gave Parker a curious squint as though asking what a Texas Ranger was doing in Arkansas.

"This here is Texas Ranger Luke Dunn Junior," he said, with emphasis on "Junior."

A flash of recognition swept across Reeves's face. "You the son of..." His voice trailed off.

"Yes sir, Marshal Reeves," I responded.

He broke his stern aura. "That's Deputy Marshal Reeves, Ranger Dunn," he corrected.

I almost reflexively responded by correcting his truncating of Texas Ranger. "Yes, sir, Deputy Marshal Reeves. It's a pleasure to meet you."

"How can I help you?" asked Reeves in a deep baritone voice.

"Texas Ranger Dunn's father suggested he seek out your advice on a case he's trying to solve," interrupted Judge Parker. He looked from Reeves to me and gave a knowing smile. "I'll let you two chat. I've got legal business to tend to. I must confirm the executed man's death." With that, Parker ambled off toward the gallows, where Casharego's deceased body was already propped up on a board for public display. They had the decency to close the deceased man's eyes and stuff his tongue back in his mouth. Onlookers filed by, attracted like ants to a honey pot.

"Let's grab a seat over yonder," said Reeves with a motion to a bench set under a shade tree.

I dutifully followed. It had already struck me that he was a big man, perhaps an inch shorter than me but broader across the shoulders. "I hear tell you've had success arresting wanted men mostly up in the Oklahoma Territory," I ventured in a vain attempt to begin a conversation.

Reeves said nary a word. He took a seat on the bench, leaned back, and tipped his hat lower on his forehead. He appeared quite relaxed. I'd learn that was an affectation he practiced.

I sat beside Reeves.

"Tell me what you're dealing with Luke," he'd suddenly shifted to a more familiar mode of address. "Oh, and feel free to call me Bass," he added. "I only use titles around the judge." An easy smile broke out beneath his big mustache.

I explained as much as I knew about the case in Kerrville, including the warnings and my suspicion of being spied upon.

Reeves nodded thoughtfully with each fact.

"That's about all," I concluded.

"Patience," Reeves said with that smooth baritone of his.

I gave him a curious look.

"It's going to take patience, Luke. Plus, you have a lot of digging yet to do." He paused to let that sink in.

"What sort of digging?"

"You say the victims owned land near this Kilkenny fellow. Has he acquired any of their holdings? If he's involved in the killings, I suspect the man will wait a respectable time before he makes any move. You'll have to keep an eye out for any deed transfers at the courthouse." Reeves tipped his hat back. "You might also look into which other landowners of adjoining properties might be targets for getting chiseled out of their ranches."

I was becoming all-too-aware of what Reeves meant by patience. "But I don't think Kilkenny is likely to be the killer."

"He may have nothing to do with the killings," mused Reeves. He froze in deep thought. "My bones are telling me that the person behind the murders will be someone you'd never suspect."

"So, you're figuring that I should do some more digging at the courthouse and then keep an eye on the owners of the ranches that are most likely to fall victim?"

"That's about the size of it. As to this Archie Parr fellow, I don't expect his type would get mixed up in killings. Nothing like a murder trial to mess up a political career." Reeves smiled again. "Oh, and I wouldn't discount the involvement of this Kilkenny fella's daughter. If she's the sort of flirty vixen you described, she could be in on it."

I questioned myself as to why I hadn't come up with the approach Reeves had laid out.

"Don't beat yourself up, Luke. Sometimes, it just takes another set of thinking to come up with a plan. I expect you might find yourself one of these days giving someone the same advice."

Hearing Reeves's point of view was sort of refreshing. It

sure caused me to realize how much I yet had to learn about being an effective lawman. "I appreciate your advice, Bass."

"Well, Luke, I hope I've been helpful. I must get along. I have a couple of warrants to deliver tomorrow." He stood, and I arose beside him. "Give my best to your father. From what Judge Parker told me, he was a legendary Texas Ranger. And best of luck to you, son."

We shook hands, and Reeves headed off. He paused and gave me a thoughtful look. "Always expect the unexpected," he said with a smile. "And don't be afraid to try the unexpected yourself." He walked off as smoothly as any man I'd ever seen. His natural stride was such that he'd likely have put a Comanche hunter to shame. Our meeting had been brief, almost anticlimactic in a sense. I had the feeling I hadn't seen the last of Bass Reeves.

As I strode away, I caught what I thought was a flat-brimmed black hat among the crowd. Was it my train companion? Coincidence? I scanned the crowd, but the hat had disappeared.

I reckoned to spend the night at the Lindell Hotel and catch the train the next morning. That gave me pause to wonder whether my black-hatted companion would be heading back on the same train?

The desk clerk was polite enough, once again suggesting that I sample the "desserts" of Fort Smith. Naturally, I declined. I reckoned I had enough of extracurricular intentions on my hands having to deal with Diana Kilkenny. I decided to pack it in, as the train would depart early.

ELEVEN
A SUSPECT?

WELL, I'll be! The man with the black hat stood at the far end of the platform, leaning against the station wall with one foot planted against it. If he had an interest in me, he was working right hard not to show it. For the first time, I noted that he was packing a gun. From a distance, it looked to be an 1890 Colt Single Action Army 1st Generation Revolver. It appeared to be the .38 caliber edition. The gun hung in a holster hung low on his hip. I asked myself why the change? I didn't recall him carrying a weapon on the trip to Fort Smith. It sort of raised my hackles a tad, and put me on high alert to be sure. I reflexively rubbed the butt of the Smith & Wesson in my holster.

The train charged into the station amid a cacophony of squealing brakes and blasts of steam. As I placed my foot on the ladder to climb aboard, I saw my black-hatted companion climb aboard at the rear of the last coach. I stepped back and watched the train pull out. There'd be another in a couple of hours.

For the first time, I drew an expression from the black-hatted stranger. It was consternation. If he was following me, and I'm sure he was, he'd been hoodwinked. I'd outwitted him for now. It remained to be seen whether he'd be waiting for me at the Marshall train station.

I bought a newspaper and awaited the next train.

The black-hatted stranger was no dummy. He wasn't on the platform to greet me in Marshall. If he was what I figured him to be, he'd surely reveal himself soon enough.

The trip to Longview was short. I stretched my legs on the depot platform, but the black-hatted spy was nowhere to be seen. He was a cagey one, to be certain. Then again, had he given up? Was I being paranoid?

It was a long ride to Palestine. I read the newspaper twice, boring myself to sleep. The shuddering of the train as it pulled into Palestine awakened me. I looked out the window, as the train approached the platform.

Well, I wasn't to be disappointed. The black-hatted stranger was sitting on a bench, crossed legs stretched out in front of him, and hat tilted low over his eyes. I decided to be bold. There was no point in pussy-footing around. There was no question that he'd been following me. The why in my head screamed for an answer.

I unfastened the strap securing my gun and headed straight for him. As I approached, he did the darndest thing. He pulled an envelope from his vest. I was within a couple of feet from him and about to speak, when he thrust the envelope up at me. His steely-eyed gaze told me to take it.

In the time it took for me to take the envelope, open it, and begin to read the scrawl on the note within, I looked up to see an empty bench. He'd disappeared pretty much right before my very eyes. If he'd had any ill intent, he could have plugged me then and there. I shook my head. I'd been careless.

There I was, holding a letter in my hand and staring at the station wall. I looked back at the note and whispered its words. "Mr. Texas Ranger, Stay off this case. I could easily have killed you. This is your final warning. Garth Jones." Garth Jones? A threat for sure. Was this the name of the black-hatted stranger or someone else? In all my travels, I'd never heard of a Garth Jones.

In any case, the man was gone. I did a quick search of the depot grounds, but he was nowhere to be seen. All I could do now was await the train to Corpus Christi where I'd be reunited with Tornado and head on home. I reckoned to check with the sheriff in Corpus to see whether he'd heard of this Garth Jones fellow. Was he a serious threat?

Upon arrival in Corpus, I fetched Tornado and headed to the sheriff's office. John McTiernan had replaced my cousin Pat Whelan. I fondly recalled that Whelan had teamed with another cousin, Texas Ranger Red John Dunn, to fend off an attack on Corpus Christi by Mexican bandits back in 1875. It was called the Good Friday Raid, or alternatively the Nuecestown Raid. The posse managed to free hostages and chase off the bandits with the loss of only one posse member. Red John described being in the midst of the melee as bullets buzzed everywhere. They'd have finished off the bandits but for the posse running out of ammunition. I was a mere six years old at the time, but heard the tale many times. My dad always regretted missing out on the excitement, as he'd been caught up with other matters at the time.

I knocked at McTiernan's office door and was invited in.

"Well, if it isn't Luke Dunn's boy," he declared. "How you be, son? Texas Ranger now, are yuh? Reckon the fruit falls close to the tree."

I expect I was destined to live with the comparisons to my father. "Good morning, Sheriff." I spied a carafe of coffee close by. "May I?"

McTiernan nodded. "What are you up to?"

I poured a cup of coffee, took a sip, and nearly spit it out. "I'm working a murder case up in Kerrville at Captain Hughes's direction. You ever hear of a fellow named Garth Jones?"

"Garth! Whoee! He's one mean wrangler, Junior. I hear tell he's killed at least a dozen, mostly ne-er do wells that needed killing." McTiernan got up and poured himself a cup of coffee. He took a swig and spat it out. "How can you drink this swill?" he asked, then laughed upon realizing it was the coffee he'd himself brewed.

"What's he look like?" I asked.

"Slender fellow. Sinister eyes. Always wears a broad-brimmed black hat. Carries an 1890 Colt Single Action."

"Damn!" I nearly shouted. "The sonofabitch followed me all the way to Fort Smith and back. Handed me a threatening note up in Palestine and disappeared."

"You're a lucky man, Junior. I never heard of the likes of Garth Jones issuing warnings," observed McTiernan.

"Someone wants me off the Kerrville matter," I postulated.

"I'd be watching your backtrail, Junior. Don't go messing with Jones."

"I'm curious as to who hired him?" I mused.

"From what I've heard, it'd take big money to hire him. Word is he never misses," advised McTiernan.

"Could he be involved in the killings on the Guadalupe?" I ventured.

"Bushwhacking ain't his style, Junior," noted McTiernan. "And he prefers that fine Colt he carries to a rifle. I think he likes the action up close and personal. I even heard that he knifed one victim to death."

So much for my theory that Jones was a spy. He was apparently far more than that. "Well, I appreciate the information, Sheriff. Guess I'll be moseying home then head to Kerrville."

"Give my best to your father," McTiernan offered in closing.

I headed out, scanned the street, and mounted Tornado. I looked forward to a night at home before returning to help Sheriff Vann.

With the prospect of possibly a month ahead of me in Kerrville, I reckoned to make sure the night with my Cassie would be memorable. It was far-too-chilly to enjoy our favorite pool at the creek, but passions could more than compensate for the setting. As I neared Heaven's Gate, I tried to divest myself of thoughts of Garth Jone's threat. Nevertheless, it hung around me. I didn't envision some sort of fast-draw gunfight in the street as depicted in those dime-store rags, but reckoned that I was likely to have to face Jones at some point.

As I turned to the gate, the action of a rifle lever hit my ears. I dove from the saddle, as a bullet ricocheted from the wrought-iron gateway. "Who goes!" I demanded. Silence. I heard a horse's hoofbeats fade away. Was it another fake bushwhacking aimed at scaring me off?

I have no idea why, but I found myself wondering whether Diana Kilkenny might be behind this. I recalled

Bass Reeves suggesting that I not overlook her. I got up, dusted myself off, and climbed back into the saddle.

I found myself angry. I sure didn't appreciate being threatened. I spurred Tornado into a canter and was soon leading him into his stall. I curried him a bit roughly, and he informed me of his displeasure with a nip at my arm. I needed to get my head together. I made my peace with Tornado, washed the trail dust from my face and hands, and headed to the house.

Cassie was fiddling with pie fixings, as I entered the kitchen. The hug delivered with her flour-covered hands left white handprints on the shoulders of my dark-blue shirt. Her lips left no residue other than passion. "Welcome home, Lucas," she cooed, wiping her hands on her apron.

I pulled her in and held her tightly. "Been a tough couple of days, sweetheart."

"Well, tell me all about it. Did you meet Marshal Reeves?"

I pulled up a chair at the kitchen table, and she sat beside me with her hands on my arm. I winced a bit, as she grabbed the precise spot Tornado had nipped. "I met Judge Parker and he introduced me to Reeves." I decided not to mention that we witnessed a hanging. "Reeves heard me out and offered some advice. Some of it validated what I'd already been thinking, but he was helpful. He didn't think Archie Parr would be involved and suggested that I find out what other properties might be targets of what appears to be a landgrabber."

Cassie gave me that look that said I wasn't telling everything.

I swallowed hard. "A fellow followed me to Fort Smith and back. He gave me a threatening note when we returned, then disappeared. Sheriff McTiernan says the man is a notorious gunman named Garth Jones. I think Jones sent some messages to whoever is behind the murders and landgrabs. He warned me to stay away from Kerrville."

"What else?" Cassie had a way of drawing truths from me.

"Somebody took a shot at me as I entered Heaven's Gate, then rode off. I think they missed intentionally."

Cassie smiled winsomely. "And?"

"Reeves told me not to overlook Kilkenny's daughter as possibly involved in the killings."

Cassie slid over into my lap. "I love you, Lucas Dunn." Our hands were just getting busy, when a plaintive cry came from the nursery. "Let me feed Sean," whispered Cassie. "Then..." She slid from my lap and padded to the nursery.

I figured she'd be a few minutes so I strode over to the pantry. I reckoned that dinner wasn't on our schedule. I opened the pantry door and was greeted by a couple of those bear sign she'd learned to bake. I snuck a few bites before heading to our bedroom.

★★

After a night of unbridled lovemaking, the toughest thing in my world was to have to leave. I lay in bed a few moments, savoring Cassie's head nestled against my chest and the aroma of her perfume filling my senses. She was warm. We were both naked with a light cotton sheet partially covering us. I turned my head to take in the curves of her hips and breasts and craved taking her once more before I departed.

She opened her eyes and caught the desire in mine. Her free hand caressed my chest, moving ever-so-slowly to my rising manhood. Her tongue tickled my ear, then her lips followed her hand. Far too quickly, we were caught up in the rapture that seemed ever ours to enjoy. It sure was an incredibly wonderful way to begin our day.

Lovemaking over, I chuckled at the fact that I was going to be leaving late for Kerrville. There was no question in my mind that savoring passions with my beautiful wife was well worth the delay. Cassie went off to feed Sean before whipping up a breakfast worthy of a husband about to be off fulfilling his lawman duties.

As I sat sipping coffee, I couldn't take my eyes off her. With hands that had but an hour before roamed my body, she deftly moved the spatula among the eggs in the frying pan. Venison sausages sizzled alongside. Yep, Cassie was as fine a woman as could be found. Even the bulge forming at her belly gave her an allure, a sexiness, that I found captivating.

Cassie poured more coffee, filled two plates, and we sat close as lovers dared without distraction from devouring breakfast.

She went to fill a bag with some bear sign to take on the trail. She opened the pantry door and gave me a suspicious glance and wink upon seeing that I'd already shorted her one. She ambled over and sat in my lap with her arms wrapped around me and a passionate kiss from her lips. She finally sighed and pulled away. "Go saddle up, Mr. Texas Ranger."

Tornado sensed the adventure ahead, as I saddled him up. A little prancing and nickering accompanied, nuzzling me excitedly. We'd travel light with only a bedroll and what I could pack in my oversized saddlebags. I had no idea how long we'd be away. Bass Reeves and my dad had both counseled patience. I had a lot of work ahead of me, mostly digging into county records. I still had no real suspect, though motive was evolving in my mind.

I did find space in my saddlebag for the *Huckleberry Finn*

book. I was curious to get into it. Like *The Red Badge of Courage* novel Kilkenny had loaned me, I reckoned there was some sort of underlying meaning he was trying to communicate. The Crane book had offered an introspective point of view. I rather expected the Mark Twain book would contrast with broader worldviews.

I held Sean, letting his tiny hands stroke my face. Then, I hugged Cassie tightly, and we parted with a deep kiss. I slowly climbed into the saddle and gave her as loving a look as I could muster. It wasn't hard to do.

I headed toward Nuecestown from where I'd head westward up the south bank of the Nueces River to the Pinta Trail. I had about six days ahead of me, if I pushed hard. I pulled *Huckleberry Finn* from my saddlebag and gave Tornado his head.

I was so engrossed in the book, that I barely paid attention to folks as we rode through Nuecestown. I did look up a couple of times to acknowledge old friends and note that the town seemed to be dying. The railroad had passed it by, an economic death knell to many old west towns.

I'm not the fastest reader, so *Huckleberry Finn* would take a couple of days. I did remain somewhat vigilant to my surroundings. Maybe it was an overreactive imagination on my part, but I sensed that I was being followed. Garth Jones? Maybe.

I wrapped up reading *Huckleberry Finn* on the morning of the third day. I found the story fascinating in the tale of two boys rafting down the Mississippi River, encountering racism, violence, hypocrisy, and more. It mirrored the panoply of evils I'd already observed in my brief life. I enjoyed the way Twain captured the lingo, the way folks talked. I also appreciated the satire embedded in his humor. Returning the books would afford me an opportunity to see

Kilkenny, and I reckoned a conversation about the books would ensue.

As I rode up the Pinta Trail, I enjoyed the Texas vistas. Cattle and horses gazed at us from behind barbed wire fences. In most places, roads had replaced rough trails, and bridges traversed creeks and washes. I kept an eye on my backtrail but saw nothing. I even doubled back a time or two, but came up empty. If Jones was still tailing me, he was very good at it. I patted the Big Fifty in the saddle scabbard. I still had my trusty lever-action 1895 Winchester, but brought the Sharps along just in case I found a need for greater firepower. Twice I had cause to put my Smith & Wesson into action against rattlesnakes that slithered a tad too close for comfort. Yes, I cooked one up for dinner. Rattlesnake meat is a right delicious treat with the right spices tossed in. I'd eaten gator a time or two down around Corpus Christi, but found rattler to be more tender to my palate.

The heat of mid-August was as oppressive as ever. I kept my bandana wrapped around my neck and soaked, as the evaporation had a cooling effect. It wasn't enough. I think my sweat was sweating. The possibility that Garth Jones was stalking me weighed heavily and likely added to the wilting heat hanging upon me.

I was riding the south bank of the Guadalupe River about a day out of Kerrville, when I decided to rest Tornado and take a load off myself. The water was cool relative to the air, so I pulled off my boots and waded out a few feet. Fortunately, and despite the sweltering heat, I kept my gun belt strapped on. The gun was heavy, but I reckoned I couldn't be too careful.

Tornado was slurping up water while I dipped my bandana in the river, when I heard the telltale click of a rifle lever. Trust me, any seasoned lawman knows the sound. I felt a chill work its way up my spine. I flattened myself on the riverbank. Water oozed its way into my boots and began to wick its way up my pant leg. My senses came alive.

I saw the muzzle flash before the explosion rocked the landscape. A bullet whizzed harmlessly past my head and into a nearby tree. Was it another fake ambush or a lousy shot? This was getting old. Once again, the sound of hoofbeats trailed off into the distance.

The question of who was behind this became ever more constant on my mind. Did I have a suspect right under my very nose and was blinded to whoever it was? With a resigned shrug, I mounted up to continue my journey to Kerrville.

A couple of hours later, fate did shine upon me. A javelina wandered across the trail with his brood. They're nasty-looking creatures and give off an aroma that could shame a skunk. Their dispositions tended to be nasty as well. This was a job for my Winchester, and I quickly dispatched dinner. The pig's brethren scampered off, and I dismounted and field-dressed the beast. I wrapped my bandana over my nose to better endure the odor. Eventually, I carved out some meat worthy of cooking and putting in my stomach. This incident nearly brought me to a sense of normalcy, though I still focused on the murder case.

TWELVE
BACK TO KERRVILLE

THE SUN SENT shards of light into my face, as I slowly awakened to the sounds of cattle mooing and bawling. I reckoned that I must have camped near a ranch. It had been dark when I bedded down.

Sure enough, I stood and gazed out at some hundred or so head of cattle pastured a hundred yards off. There were no wranglers around, so I figured the beeves had moved on their own to satisfy their thirsts.

I saddled Tornado, mounted up, and started on the last leg of my ride to Kerrville. I admittedly asked myself what my fake bushwhacker had in store for me today. By taking a single shot and running, he sure wasn't using much ammunition. I permitted myself a chuckle, though dared not lose my cautionary edge.

Sheriff Vann's office soon came into sight. I reckoned he might be just a tad impatient at my extended absence. I reined in at the jail and bounded up the steps, pausing just long enough to knock and await an invitation.

"Come on in," came Vann's voice.

I stepped through the door and stood silently, waiting

for Vann to look up from his desk. I stood there for at least a minute, shifting weight from one foot to the other and scanning the rack of rifles and shotguns behind the sheriff's desk.

Vann finally looked up. His jaw dropped at the sight of me. "Damn, but it's about time, Ranger." His brows furrowed as he pointed to the chair near his desk. "Set a spell and make me believe you've been doin' something productive on this case."

I spun the chair so the back was toward him and slung my frame into the seat. I tipped back my hat and folded my arms on the top of the chair back. I tried to muster as intensely serious an expression as I could manage. I proceeded to relate my meeting with Archie Parr, encounters with Garth Jones, the bushwhacker that kept missing, meeting with Bass Reeves, and threatening messages.

"And what am I supposed to conclude from all of this, Ranger?"

"I've got a lot of work to do at the courthouse and then need to connect the dots."

Vann shook his head. He rightly figured that I hadn't gotten very far toward solving the murders.

"I have my suspicions," I offered.

"You sharing them?" Vann asked.

"Just as soon hold my cards close right now, Sheriff." I knew Vann wouldn't like this answer at all, but for all I knew, even he could have some connection. He's already been on the scene for one murder, and he was the tax collector, so he would know the ownership status of properties around Kerr County.

Vann raised one eyebrow. "What would your dad have done?" he challenged me.

I smiled. "Actually, I'm following his advice."

The sheriff leaned back in his chair with hands folded behind his head. What could he say?

"What do you know about that Garth Jones fellow I mentioned? Sheriff McTiernan down Nueces County way told me that Jones was a gun for hire who'd killed nearly a dozen men."

Vann sat upright, rifled through a stack of papers, pulled one out, and pushed it across the desk at me. "See for yourself."

Turned out that Vann was wanted for a litany of crimes, including rustling, robbery, and murder. "Impressive. You figuring to arrest him?"

The sheriff shook his head dismayingly. "If I see his face in Kerr County and have a passel of deputies with me, I just might take him on."

I stood and spun the chair back around. I gave the sheriff a penetrating look. "I stood face-to-face with him back in Palestine, Sheriff. He was standing closer than you and me right here and now. His venomous presence and the darkness surrounding him would put a rattlesnake to shame." I looked about as intensely as I could at the sheriff. "If we meet again, one of us will surely die. I don't intend for it to be me."

Vann relaxed. "I'm glad to have you back, Dunn. Do what you must do to solve this damned case. Folks are crawling up my butt over it."

I could imagine the pressure he must be under. "I'd best get to my job, Sheriff. I'll check with you when I know something more solid." My mind was already paying a visit to Kilkenny. I did have to return his books and pass along Archie Parr's regards.

★★

Upon leaving Vann, I found my way to the stable. I reckoned Tornado had earned himself a good currying and some sweet treats.

"Howdy, Ranger. Good to see yuh back," welcomed the stable hand. "Been another killin' while yuh bin gone."

"So I hear," I said with a covert-looking look. "You solved them yet?" I teased. Timmy wasn't exactly playing with a full deck upstairs, but he was a good kid with nary a bad bone in his body.

"I think it be Mexkin bandits," offered Timmy with a confidential tone. "Them bean-eaters bin nosin' 'round."

I tried to appear to take him seriously.

"Can't be no injuns. They take hair," he added with assurance.

"Well, you keep your eyes open, Timmy." I looked down the street at the clock in front of the courthouse. I figured that midday was as good a time as any to pay a visit to Kilkenny. I was about to head over to the hotel restaurant to grab a bite, when Timmy grabbed my arm.

He leaned into me with his hand partially covering his mouth as though fixing to deliver a secret. "That there Garth Jones took him a hoss but an hour ago, Ranger Dunn," he said in a low, confidential tone. "Headed that way." He pointed a finger west toward Kilkenny's place.

I nearly lost my appetite. What might Jones be up to? I'd been warned. Was he going to deliver on his threat? Was he aiming to make me number twelve? Who was paying him? What had my dad and Bass Reeves advised? Patience. "I'll be back in an hour, Timmy."

It seemed appropriate to deal with this situation on a full stomach. It would buy me time to cogitate on how best to deal with Jones. If he was intending to set an ambush, I had to outthink him. If he had to wait, it just might make him impatient. That could work in my favor. I hoisted my saddlebags over my shoulder, grabbed my rifles, and headed to the restaurant. It was a tad early. As I entered the dining room and scanned the room, I gave a nod to a couple of older citizens setting about drinking coffee. I grabbed a seat near a window with a view to the street. I was hidden from street view by a diaphanous curtain but able to see through it.

It was still early enough, so I ordered up eggs, pork sausage, and biscuits with steaming hot, fresh-brewed coffee. The server was a lovely young Mexican lass named Esmeralda.

Soon enough, Esmeralda placed a delectable-looking feast before me. "You are Ranger, *señor*?" she ventured.

I nodded, as I shoved a forkful of eggs into my mouth. I was hungrier than I'd realized. "*Si*," I responded between chews.

"*Usted en peligro, señor*," she warned with a near whisper. "*Malas personas.*"

Well, I knew I was in danger. Timmy had me alert to that. "*¿Cómo lo sabes?*"

"*Dice el hombre malvado*," she advised.

Trying to act nonchalant, I stuffed a piece of sausage in my mouth. "*¿Quién?*" I asked.

Esmeralda shrugged. "*Sin nombre. Usa sombrero negro.*" She couldn't give me a name, but she'd given a hint that it was Garth Jones. "*Y un arma grande.*"

A well-armed man wearing a black hat sounded suspiciously like Jones. "*¿Cuando?*" I asked.

She blushed a little and glanced furtively toward the kitchen. "*Ayer por la noche.*" She was embarrassed that she'd learned this during the night. It seemed that Esmeralda was more than a restaurant server.

"*Muchasi gracias*," I replied. "*Nunca lo diré.*" I promised that I'd never tell about her evening liaison.

"*Buena suerte, señor.*" I watched her turn and gracefully head back to the kitchen.

Good luck, indeed.

As I took a final sip of coffee, a movement outside caused me to glance out the window. Diana Kilkenny rode by. I had to admit that she sat a fine saddle. She was an alluring little filly, but gave off more danger signs than a nest of rattlesnakes. It gave me to wonder whether she'd be at Kilkenny's ranch when I visited.

I looked over at the clock on the mahogany mantle over the fireplace that took up a good portion of one end of the dining room. It was getting to be near eleven o'clock. What with keeping a wary eye out for Jones, I reckoned it'd take a good hour to ride out the Kilkenny's place.

THIRTEEN

FOIL A BUSHWHACKER

TIMMY HAD Tornado saddled and ready to ride about the time I arrived at the stable.

"Reckoned you'd be back in an hour," he advised.

"Thanks," I said and placed a silver dollar in his hand. "I'll keep a sharp eye out for Jones," I assured him. I slung the saddlebags behind Tornado's saddle and tied them down. Next came the Sharps carbine and the Winchester. I expect I appeared about ready for most any trouble.

Timmy nodded and smiled as he handed me the reins.

I mounted up and headed Tornado west at a walk. Patience. The word kept rumbling about in my brain. I did have enough quiet time at the restaurant to give plenty of thought to how to best take on Garth Jones. My dad and I had been on plenty of hunts with our old mountain man friend Buffalo Watts. Watts taught me most of what could be taught about tracking. I stopped at the edge of town and dismounted. I stripped off anything that jingled, especially my spurs. I was concerned about squeaking leather, so laid in a bit of bear grease where I could find spots that tended to rub noisily. I doffed my boots and slipped on a pair of moccasins. I remounted. Instead of following the road that led to Kilkenny's place, I took to the south bank of the Guadalupe, which tended to feature some high bluffs as I headed upstream. It was roughly eight miles to Kilkenny's ranch. My intuition told me that if Jones was fixing to bushwhack me, he'd most likely be further from Kerrville.

I'd ridden about halfway to Kilkenny's, making a trail where there was none. I stayed away from the places where the bluffs overlooked the river, as it would make me an easy target for anyone lurking on the north bank. Then again, Jones could as easily be lying in wait somewhere ahead of me along the south bank.

I dismounted and slipped the Winchester from its scabbard. I'd be on foot from here on. Now, my tracking skills had to come into full play. My life depended on it. It was still hotter than Hades, but a misty rain coated the landscape such that my steps and those of Tornado were muffled. Nevertheless, I trod as softly as possible. A snapped twig could doom me, if in fact, Jones was out there waiting for me. I stopped every few yards to scan the area with my sharp vision as honed on years of hunting game.

With a seventy-five to hundred or more field of vision on either side of me, I trod a zig-zag pattern, taking close to an hour to move a mere half mile. The Guadalupe was always on my right and an old road on my left. There was no shortage of places for a bushwhacker to lie in ambush. I studied the landscape with the practiced eye of a hunter. A bushwhacker would just have to wait long enough to put his sights on the back of his prey. Patience was still critically important. Would my patience outlast Jones? By my reckoning, the hunter had become the hunted.

Wind stirred clumps of grass and rattled the rain-laden tree leaves.

It's amazing how something as simple as a broad-brimmed black hat can be overlooked. I crested a rise and gazed down below. Setting there perhaps fifty feet ahead of me was a black hat. Yep, it was Garth Jones kneeling with his Sharps nestled in the crotch of a tree and barrel pointed in the general direction of the road below him. His gaze was fixed on the road.

There was no point in alerting him unnecessarily by taking another step. I brought my Winchester up and aimed carefully. "Garth Jones, you reckoning to size up grave space?" I said while chambering a round.

His face was hidden from me, but I could see Jones's shoulders hunch with surprise. His mouth surely gaped.

"Take your hands from that carbine, Jones. Stand up, raise your hands high, and turn slowly toward me."

Jones exhaled audibly and did as he was told. Now, he was in the position of judging whether he could drop his hands, pull a gun, and fire quickly enough to beat my index finger wrapped on the trigger of my trusty Winchester.

"Come toward me ten steps." I was determined to get him away from the Sharps carbine. I reckoned him to be smart enough to not go for the Colt in his holster.

Again, he did as he was told. He looked up at me. "You're damned good, Ranger Dunn."

"Drop your left hand and drop the gun belt." I wasn't about to be distracted by any chatter, especially compliments.

Jones unfastened the buckle and let the gun belt drop to the ground. I could see a trickle of sweat run down his cheek.

"Now, real easy-like, remove the little pocket pal from your vest and let it drop."

Jones gave me a damning look and slipped the Derringer from his pocket and let it drop. He gave me an "are you satisfied" look.

I shook my head. "You play me for a fool, Garth Jones? Let your Bowie knife join the Derringer." So far as I could figure, he was disarmed.

"Can we talk Ranger?" Here it was coming. The slick-talking devil was going to try to talk his way out. "I know what this looks like, but I was only going to fire a warning shot to scare you off."

Setting for a couple of hours in this heat accompanied by an earlier misty rain was a pretty elaborate setup for a mere warning shot. "Afraid I'm not buying that, Jones." I kept my rifle trained on him. "Where's your horse?"

He motioned up the trail with a nod of his head.

"Well, you just march yourself toward your mount. Walk slowly or I'll give you a hitch in your get-along that you won't soon forget. As to trying to get away, don't try it. I can knock the eyes out of a squirrel at fifty yards." As Jones began walking toward his horse, I picked up his weapons and shoved all but the Sharps into my saddlebags.

As Jones walked in front of me, I was able to take in how wiry but apparently well-muscled he was. I dared take no chances. We were about fifteen feet from his horse and near a large tree. "Stop!" I ordered. I wiped sweat from my brow. Dang, but it was hot and terribly humid.

Jones complied.

"Face that tree and place your hands on it as high as you can reach. Spread your legs and lean into the tree." This would be Jones's only chance to escape. I was taller and heavier-muscled than he, so he was surely calculating his chances of out-muscling me. I came up close with my Smith & Wesson in my left hand, grabbed his right hand, and snapped one cuff on his wrist with a satisfying click as it locked. Now, Jones stood facing the tree with one hand cuffed and the other grabbing tree bark. I had a grip on the second cuff strand but had the dilemma of holding the gun in my left hand. I had no choice but to holster my trusty revolver.

Jones heard the gun slide into my holster. I was close enough to feel him flinch.

Reflexively, I kicked his left leg out wider, putting him off balance.

"Damn you, Ranger," snarled Jones.

I brought his left hand down and now had his hands cuffed behind his back.

"Ain't getting me on that hoss," he said tauntingly.

I spun him around to face me. "Ride, walk, or be dragged, you're going to jail in Kerrville," I assured him.

"What's your charge? You got nothing on me that you can make stick. I was only hunting out here."

"I'm charging you with attempted murder, Garth Jones. One way or another, you'll set a spell in one of Sheriff Vann's cells for a day or so." I gave him a hard look. I wanted to plant him in a cell at least temporarily, so I could visit Kilkenny with peace of mind. "You going the easy way or the hard way?"

Jones sighed resignedly. "I'll ride."

I secured him in his saddle, tying him to the fenders. I then tied a long tether to his horse's bridle and mounted Tornado. I figured the ride to Kerrville and jailing Jones should go swiftly enough to leave plenty of time to visit Kilkenny. I had an ace up my sleeve. Unbeknownst to Jones, Sheriff Vann held a wanted poster on him.

I pushed Jones roughly through the door of the Kerrville jail. There were a few gawkers standing nearby. One or two likely knew of Jones and offered knowing smiles.

"What the hell?" exclaimed Vann with enough surprise to nearly tip over in his chair.

"I'm arresting Garth Jones here for attempted murder, Sheriff."

"I didn't attempt to murder anybody, Sheriff. I was just hunting. Never even fired a shot."

"He was laying on the trail waiting to ambush me. I have his threatening note to prove his intent."

"You got thin air, Ranger," said a glowering Jones.

Vann smiled. "You saved me a lot of trouble, Ranger Dunn."

Jones gave a questioning look.

I smiled knowingly.

Sheriff Vann opened a desk drawer and drew out a yellow wanted poster. "Well, lookee here, Mr. Jones. Seems you're a wanted man in these parts. Even a reward on your head." Vann cooed at me. "Whoee, three thousand dollars!"

"Sonofabitch!" hollered Jones.

"I'll write up a report of the capture, Sheriff."

I handed Vann the key to the handcuffs, and he escorted a decidedly reluctant Garth Jones to a cell. Vann returned with my handcuffs. "Great job, Junior."

It was the first time Vann had addressed me by my nickname. I reckoned he must be warming to me. "I need to go visit Kilkenny, Sheriff. I'll get you that report later, if you don't mind?"

"Take your time. Shucks, you've made my day."

I already figured to share the reward with Vann.

FOURTEEN
DUELING PURPOSES

I RODE through the gate at Kilkenny's ranch now with a sense of accomplishment. Garth Jones shouldn't be a bother for a few years, assuming justice was served. I reckoned to do some mental exercises with Kilkenny yet admittedly dreading the prospect of his daughter being home. I had no intentions of sampling the woman's offerings, but fending her off might be no easy task.

I pretty much gave Tornado his head, as I was in no hurry. All too soon, I reined in before Kilkenny's house and scanned the area. In the few weeks I'd been away, some landscaping had been done toward prettifying the place. There were late-blooming flowers and some cacti that were struggling to survive transplanting. The front door had received a fresh coat of paint. I wondered whether the deep red color choice had any special significance. I slid from my saddle, hitched Tornado, grabbed *Huckleberry Finn* and *The Red Badge of Courage* from my saddlebags, and ambled up to the door. The paint was dry but gave off a strong, oily aroma. This was about to be displaced. Before I could knock, Diana opened the door. Her perfume wafted over me.

"Why Ranger Dunn. What a pleasant surprise," she cooed with a smile across her luscious red lips. A red that put the door to shame.

Maybe I was over-sensitive, but her greeting lingered too long on "surprise." I doffed my hat. "I'm pleased to see you, too, Diana. Is your father at home?"

She batted her long eyelashes at me. "Why yes. I believe he's in the library." She glanced deferentially at the two books I was carrying. She turned and motioned me to follow. "I do hope you can stay for dinner," she invited with a flirtatious look over her shoulder. She knocked on the library door. "Father, Texas Ranger Dunn is here to see you."

"Hrumph! Send him in," came the reply.

I eased my way past Diana, though she made certain that I'd have to brush against her breasts as I squeezed by. Her perfume nearly overwhelmed my senses.

"I'll see you later," she whispered provocatively and glided her way up the hall. I couldn't help but steal a look at her shapely figure.

"You here to see me or my daughter?" came a witty query from Kilkenny. He picked up the cigar box and offered me a smoke knowing that I never partook.

I blushed a tad at Kilkenny's wry humor referencing Diana, placed the two books on the desk, and took a seat.

Kilkenny lit up and lofted a couple of smoke rings skyward. "You enjoy those books?"

I nodded. "I especially appreciated Crane's book, *The Red Badge of Courage*, as it so deeply touched on the cruelties of war." I had repeatedly practiced what I figured to tell Kilkenny. "The descriptions of conflict were quite striking, and I was gripped by Crane's delving into the inner workings of the main character's mind. Yet, I could tell that the author had never been in battle himself. To sum up, it was a deep study of the impact of violence on the human psyche."

Kilkenny took a leisurely pull on his cigar and sent a couple more smoke rings up. "Seems a pretty fair assessment, Lucas. What about Huck Finn?"

I was about to respond when Diana glided in with two cups of coffee. She turned a solicitous look on me and smiled. "I hope you'll join us for dinner this evening, Lucas," she purred like a feline on the prowl.

I glanced at Kilkenny who only shrugged.

Despite my misgivings, to refuse would be rather impolite. "It would be my pleasure, Miss Diana," I blurted while stifling a blush.

Diana gave a half curtsy. "We'll see you in the dining room in about an hour." She glided out with the same silken steps as when she'd entered. Just as she disappeared through the doorway and out of sight of her father, I'd swear that the extra jiggle she gave to her hips was for my benefit.

"Ahem," said Kilkenny, clearing his throat. "What about Huck Finn?"

"Twain wove a fascinating tale with *Huckleberry Finn*. I found that the story of two boys rafting down the Mississippi River encountering racism, violence, hypocrisy, and more mirrored much of what I'd already observed in my brief life. Of course, I never rafted the mighty Mississippi. I did enjoy the way Twain captured the lingo, the way folks talked. I also appreciated the satire embedded in his humor." I anticipated Kilkenny asking about any connection between the two books. "I found a fascinating link between the books in the context of Crane focusing on the violence that erupted over the concerns for racism that

Twain deals with. I gather that's why you chose those two, Joseph."

Kilkenny smiled. "You're pretty perceptive, Lucas. Truth be told, I have a history with the War Between the States that you likely don't know about." He sipped coffee and took another pull on the cigar. The tip glowed a bright orange in the dimly lit library. Another smoke ring went skyward. "I rode with a nasty bastard named William Quantrill. Yes, as a young buck, I was feeling adventurous and the aura of war lingered in the air."

"Quantrill," I echoed.

"They say that Quantrill opposed slavery at one time. That sure wasn't the case when I joined him. Everyone I knew seemed to be joining the Confederate cause. I heard that Quantrill had decided that slavery was right and boasted that the hanging of John Brown over the Harpers Ferry raid was too good an end for the man." Kilkenny took another sip of coffee. "Quantrill headed to Texas with a fellow named Marcus Gill, a slaver that I knew. Quantrill got himself mixed up with a fellow named Mayes, a man of mixed Scots-Irish and Cherokee blood who served in the 1st Cherokee Regiment in the Confederate army. Mayes taught guerrilla warfare tactics to Quantrill, including fighting from ambush, camouflage, and stealth tactics. Caught up in the fervor of the cause, Quantrill joined General Sterling Price and fought in the Battle of Wilson's Creek and First Battle of Lexington in August and September of 1861. I met Quantrill about the time he was forming up his own partisan unit out of Blue Springs, Missouri. Loyalty was demanded first and foremost of the men joining Quantrill."

I watched Kilkenny send another smoke ring aloft. It was occurring to me that humans seemed to learn evil in a similar fashion to learning good. That is, if a man believes the world is evil, he will absorb into his being all that supports that thesis. By contrast, a man that thinks the world is good will immerse himself in things like confidence, hope, and trust that support goodness. Yet, everyone is different. I grew up under the love and teachings of a man committed to truth and justice, who believed in the redemption of a man's soul. Kilkenny obviously didn't share such an upbringing. Consequently, his path was quite different from mine. I wondered whether he'd ever known love. I didn't sense that he loved himself, and that seemed essential to loving others. Kilkenny had become caught up in a world of men measuring themselves against other men, and he was determined to emerge a winner in that competition. I shifted in my chair.

Kilkenny continued. "Quantrill was fully committed to the Confederate cause. We became known as Quantrill's Raiders and were about as nasty a group as could be pulled together. Over time, we attracted the likes of the James and Younger brothers who went on to later fame as outlaws. We showed no quarter to our enemies. By way of example, we hit Lawrence, Kansas, in the summer of 1863, and killed nearly two hundred residents. That earned the wrath of the Confederate leadership, as they withdrew support from Quantrill. Our leader was undeterred, as he led us behind Confederate lines down to Sherman, Texas, where we wintered from 1863 to 1864." Kilkenny paused and took a long pull on his cigar. More smoke circles went aloft. "We attacked Fort Baxter, Kansas, and ambushed and killed nearly a hundred Union troops in the Battle of Baxter Springs. You might be surprised to know that I retched the first time I killed a man at close range. Watching a bullet destroy a man's face, seeing the contortions of excruciating pain, and hearing the final breaths was gut-wrenching even in the heat of battle. In Texas, we continued to embarrass the Confederate command by our often lawless actions. By the grace of God, I had my fill."

"What did you do?" I asked the obvious question.

"While in Texas, I'd learned about the port at Galveston. I became determined to seek my fortune there once hostilities ended. Quantrill's Raiders returned to Missouri in early 1864, but he took several of his most loyal troops east, toward Kentucky. Confederate hopes were waning. Pro-Union soldiers and hired killers tracked down and killed Quantrill and his men. It presaged the end of the war. Despite the influence of Quantrill and the savage loyalists surrounding him, I saw the ultimate demise of the Confederacy. I lit out for Galveston before Lee's surrender." Kilkenny smiled longingly and gently snuffed out his cigar in an ashtray, saving the stub to possibly be relit later.

I thought on Kilkenny's experience and tried to connect it with Crane's novel. War was surely hell. You either won or you lost. There was no in-between. And to the winner went the spoils. If Crane's book was to be believed, losers in war usually endured unspeakable hardships along with a sense of loss immersed in disgrace that would be hard to grasp by anyone not experiencing it. Families were broken. Wives lost husbands, and children lost fathers. Yet, I didn't sense any distress in Kilkenny. "I expect arrival in Galveston led you to the shipping business?" I queried.

Kilkenny smiled. "The war had ended by the time I arrived. With no income, I looked around for work. As a teen, I'd read about the notorious pirate Jean Lafitte who operated out of Galveston. His adventures on the high seas intrigued me. Those fantasies led me to sign with a crew on a merchant ship destined for Europe. Anyway, I swabbed decks, hoisted anchors, and barfed my guts out in heavy seas. But, I was free of the horrors of war. It might be said that the ship was my raft on the Mississippi." Kilkenny laughed at his own humor. "So, in answer to the question lingering in your eyes, I saw plenty of fighting, plenty of death, plenty of the ugliness of war. Stephen Crane was pretty close to describing a truth." He relit his cigar, took a couple of pulls, and blew another smoke ring. "I learned the law of the seas; I studied the business of hauling freight by ship."

I shifted uneasily.

"You ever kill a man?" asked Kilkenny.

I finished the last dredges of coffee from my cup and nodded solemnly. "Never had to kill a soul in battle, Joseph. In my profession, most killing tends to be personal. Even bushwhacking." I said that to get a reaction. There was none. "In fact, I prefer to avoid killing."

"You ever seen the expression on the face of a man run through by a knife or bayonet? It's very personal. It takes a hardening of the soul to kill another human." Kilkenny shifted in his chair.

It occurred to me that he took no pride in his service to the Confederacy. He'd experienced battles, but they were mostly one-sided. His wasn't a matter of a dozen men killed on each side and no clear winner. When Quantrill's Raiders won, his battles were more akin to massacres. Kilkenny's adventures on the seas intrigued me, especially as they led to him becoming a shipping tycoon.

"Any progress on the Kerrville matter?" he asked, shifting our conversation.

"Not any I can mention. I have some leads." I found that this conversation was giving me considerable insight into Kilkenny, but was getting me no closer to solving the killings in Kerrville. I was relieved to hear a bell, apparently a signal for dinner.

Kilkenny and I entered the dining room to encounter a table appointed with fine settings of China and silverware.

However, nothing was so fine as the vision overwhelming all else in the room. Diana Kilkenny stood demurely behind one of the chairs. Her hair fell in dark ringlets across bare shoulders. Make-up set off her eyes so as to accentuate their crystalline blueness. Her breasts threatened to burst from the bodice of her purple satin dress. With her waist cinched tightly, the folds of her dress flowed gracefully over her slim but just-curvaceous-enough hips. Diana lit the room afire with her presence.

Kilkenny paused, then strode over and seated his daughter. Something was whispered in her ear, but I hadn't a clue as to what was said.

I ambled over to the seat Kilkenny offered. It was directly across from Diana. As I sat, I couldn't help but be caught by her eyes. I felt like the fly meeting the spider. "Good evening, Miss Kilkenny," I managed to cough out.

"We have a treat, Lucas. One of our hands managed to bag a pronghorn." Kilkenny licked his lips for emphasis.

I strove to fend off Diana's sexually charged eyes by looking around the dining room. Gilt-framed paintings decorated the walls, and the richly-carved furnishings were rubbed to a high sheen and fashioned of rich-looking mahogany. To my relief, a Black server placed a bowl of soup before me. Somehow, I managed to spoon the delicious brew to my mouth without spilling a drop. All the while, Kilkenny rambled about the Bar K Ranch and Diana's eyes never left me. I could feel the heat of her gaze from a mere five feet away.

"How were your travels?" asked Diana.

I wanted to tell her that she ought to know. I sighed inwardly and politely described my time at Heaven's Gate Ranch and adventure at Fort Smith as briefly as I reckoned was necessary. I left out most details as to purposes and never mentioned Garth Jones. I figured that I wove a fairly plausible account.

"I hear that they call Judge Parker the Hanging Judge." noted Kilkenny. "Did you see a hanging?"

I caught Diana gazing at me as though she wished to hear every detail of any hanging. "Yes, did you witness one?" she asked with a certain drama to her voice.

"They hung some poor outlaw that a marshal named Bass Reeves had caught. It was conducted about as humanely as executions can be...I suppose. The man died right quickly once he stretched the rope." I was not inclined to linger on detailed descriptions like the cracking sound as the man's neck snapped with the jerk of the noose against his weight nor the condemned man's final death spasms.

"That must have been..." Diana was at a loss for an appropriate word.

I had the sense that she wanted to say the hanging was exciting or exhilarating. "It was to be the last hanging at Fort Smith." My response iced further discussion of the execution.

We turned to small talk about ranching. The pronghorn was indeed delicious, and the meal was topped off with a freshly-baked cherry pie. The pie turned out to be an adventure of sorts, as

Diana turned it into a nearly orgasmic event with her savoring of the cherry pie filling and licking her lips of cherry syrup droppings with slow motions of her tongue. She licked each of her fingers in a slow, decidedly-lustful manner that caused me a bit of discomfort beneath the table. Her behavior was punctuated with a bare foot rubbing my leg.

Kilkenny broke the spell Diana was casting. He glanced distractedly from Diana to me and back. "If y'all will excuse me, I've got some papers to tend to. Reckon to hit the hay early." He stood and bowed slightly. "You watch yourself around my daughter, Lucas," he cautioned. Did he not know of Diana's reputation? Was he truly oblivious?

I watched Kilkenny exit the dining room. There must have been some desperation or yearning in my eyes for Diana's foot ventured a bit higher up my leg.

"Are you okay, Lucas," she murmured with a breathy sigh. She tousled her hair provocatively.

I needed a diversion and needed it fast! My mind raced. Her foot explored. "Did you hear today's news from Kerrville?" I blurted urgently.

She smiled fetchingly as though oblivious to my question.

"Garth Jones was arrested and jailed."

There was no change in her expression, but her foot hesitated from its journey toward my manhood. It was pretty much the reaction I'd hoped for. Somehow, Diana Kilkenny was involved in these murders.

Diana refilled my wine flute and added a touch to her own. "The sunset should be beautiful, Lucas. Come and share it with me."

Like a dog on a leash, I followed her out to a covered veranda with a view of the western horizon. The sun would soon duck behind a distant hilltop and shed its golden glow against the light cloud cover. I didn't want to go, yet was drawn like a magnet caught in her aura.

She offered a bench and sat herself beside me, too close beside me. She clinked her flute to mine, and we both sipped. Her perfume was alluring, the heaving of her breasts enticing. A spell was being cast, and I felt powerless to resist.

I found myself feeling a tad woozy. The last thing I remembered was her hand inside my shirt, exploring my chest. Somehow, the buttons had been unfastened. I never felt her hands at my belt buckle or my gun slipping to the ground.

It was dark when I awakened. My head hurt. I was still seated on the bench—the last place I recalled being—though my shirt and pants lay wide open. A perfumed note hung from my pocket. Groggily, I read it. Scribbled in a decidedly feminine scrawl was a single word, "Amazing!" It was followed by a heart with an arrow drawn through it.

Had she snuck something into my wine? Had she used me while I was in some sort of stupor? What was her purpose? Questions lingered. Where had Kilkenny been while Diana did whatever she did? Worse for me in not knowing what she'd done, could I face Cassie? I desperately needed to get away from the Bar K.

I looked around the veranda. It sure looked different by daylight. Other than a wall that looked to be my height and a locked iron gate, the only escape was through the door that led back into the house. In my present condition, I didn't envision myself climbing over a wall or defeating a secured wrought-iron gate. I stood and teetered for a moment, steadying myself with my hand on the back of the bench. What had I done to myself? For one thing, I'd let myself be lured into the spider's web. I slipped off my boots. Jangling spurs and hard leather heels on a tile floor would not be especially stealthy.

Taking as deep a breath as my head allowed, I stepped into the house. I began to tiptoe down the hall toward the foyer. The first door I passed on my right was ajar, affording a glimpse inside. I peeked, then swung my head painfully away from what I'd seen. Diana was standing stark naked before a mirror, admiring herself. Damn, but she had an incredible body. Had I sampled it last night? I cringed in guilt at the thought. I stumbled a couple of times but made it to the foyer and potential escape. I thanked God that Kilkenny was nowhere to be seen.

I reached for the door-latch.

"You leavin' us, Lucas darlin'?" came a sultry voice behind me.

I paused and slowly turned to the voice.

Diana wore a diaphanous robe that left nothing to the imagination. Her raven locks fell in disarray over her shoulders.

I swallowed hard. "Gotta go," I managed to blurt out.

Her eyes went to my crotch. "Not all of you wants to go, Lucas," she cooed. "Are you hungry? Eggs? Bacon? Biscuits? Dessert?" Each word was aimed at drawing me in.

I fought off her enticements, following my desperate urge to escape and pushing through the door. Tornado still stood patiently hitched in front of the house. The poor cayuse had been there all night. I nearly forgot to put on my boots but a couple of rocks quickly reminded me. I paused just long enough to slip them on. Bending over sent blood to my head, and I nearly passed out. Shod, I staggered to my oh-so-beautiful and loyal horse. Praise the Lord for Tornado. I climbed into the saddle and turned him toward the ranch entrance. Unable to resist, I stole a glance over my shoulder.

"Later," mouthed Diana with a sexy wave that delivered her message.

Paroxysms of pain shot through my head with every step Tornado took. Escaping in pain was far preferable to another moment at the Bar K.

The question of what I had gotten myself into gnawed at my thoughts, as I rode on to Kerrville. My life-threatening duel with Jones paled in comparison with Diana Kilkenny's wiles.

FIFTEEN
HOMEWORK

I LAY on the bed in my hotel room, staring at the ceiling. What had Diana done to me? The uncertainty bedeviled the dickens from me. I had to know. How else could I face Cassie? I wished she were here. I wished I could express the depth of my love for her. I wished...I wished.

A knock at the door tore me from my languishing in self-doubt. "Hang on!" I called out. My head throbbed as I sat up, swung out, and pulled my boots on. I took a step toward the door, then paused and grabbed my gun rig.

"Git yer sorry ass outta bed, Dunn!" the person knocked more impatiently.

I took my sweet time buckling my gun belt. I didn't recognize the voice so was in no hurry. I managed to stumble to the door. With hand on gun butt, I opened it a crack. "Who..."

"Sam Chambliss! Now, let me in!" demanded my visitor.

I stepped back and let Chambliss enter. "What brings you here with such all-fired agitation?" I said as he stalked past me and plopped in the only chair in the room. Chambliss was a big man, roughly my height with maybe twenty more pounds. He was every inch a cattleman. Years on the range had browned and toughened his skin. Graying hair framed a wrinkle-laden face punctuated by a pair of blue eyes parted by a nose that had been busted a time or two. He came across as a no-nonsense man of the American west.

Chambliss began to calm a tad. "Sorry to intrude. Sheriff Vann said yuh were in town an' I oughtta talk with yuh. I hear tell Captain Hughes assigned yuh to solve the killin' on yonder river."

I eased my hand off my gun butt and relaxed. This was a man in trouble. "Pleased to make your acquaintance, Mr. Chambliss. Perhaps, you might start from the beginning. What's ailing you?"

"It's thet damn Kilkenny woman. She's twice tried to— how you say—seduce me into sellin' my Runnin' Circle Ranch. Fust, it was money, now her body." Chambliss's face grew momentarily dark. "My wife don't cotton to her none."

To say that I related too much of Chambliss's quandary would be mighty accurate. Of greater concern, it tended to bring together suspicions I had begun to form about Diana Kilkenny. "Kicker is that she hasn't broken any laws with you," I noted with a sorry shake of my head. Even that gentle motion reminded me that I was still dealing with the aftermath of whatever Diana had put in my wine.

"After what happened to Wilson and Waltz...well, I can't be livin' lookin' o'er my shoulder. Somebody needs to..." Chambliss left his words hanging. The tension in his face was concerning. Would such a man turn to killing to protect his family? With this man, it was hard to say.

"Well, the good news is that you're the first person that's come to me with evidence of her intentions. Right now, you have mere interest from her. She hadn't threatened you unless with the possibility of a slanderous relationship. Whether she's involved with the killings on the Guadalupe? There's no evidence linking her." In the back of my mind, I wondered what it might take to get Garth Jones to talk?

Chambliss sat stone still. He was obviously frustrated. "Could her father be settin' to this?"

"I've talked with Joseph Kilkenny. After the War Between the States, he went to sea and then built a successful shipping business. Why would he risk all that over some land-grabbing scheme? In his eyes, Diana can do no wrong. I doubt that he's aware of her intentions." I could see that I wasn't convincing Chambliss. "I reckon to do a bit of research today at the courthouse. I'm looking for a pattern of land acquisitions and what landowners might be vulnerable." I wanted to let this man know that I was proactively seeking to solve this case without letting any cats out of the bag. "I appreciate you coming to me, Mr. Chambliss. I'll be back with you soon." I figured it was time to end this impromptu meeting and get to my research at the courthouse.

Chambliss sighed quite audibly. He was still frustrated, but I sensed a slight easing of his tensions. "Thanks fer yer time, Ranger. Sorry to wake yuh."

"Er, do you have children?" My inquiry aimed to figure whether Chambliss had any heirs.

"Two boys," responded Chambliss. "One had his own spread down near the King Ranch, the other is studying law back east."

"You ought to be right proud. I hope my children do so well."

"Thanks. I 'preciate yuh hearin' me out," offered Chambliss. He stood, looked hopefully at me, and headed to the door.

"No problem. I'll be in touch," I said, as I opened the door to let Chambliss leave. Once he was gone, I sat on the edge of the bed to gather my thoughts. Chambliss had given me my first hint of what might be going on and who might be at the root of it all. I reckoned to grab breakfast and head to the courthouse.

"Did Sam catch up with you?" asked Martha as she placed a steaming cup of coffee before me. She was a sweetheart who'd already outlived two husbands and now made ends meet serving meals to hotel guests.

I savored a sip of coffee. "Yep, sure did," I replied.

"Special today is sausage and eggs with honey-glazed biscuits."

I nodded. "Sounds great." I sensed that she was curious about my conversation with Chambliss, but I wasn't about to satisfy her curiosity. Chambliss had come to me in confidence and didn't need his problems thrown into the Kerrville gossip mill. I took another sip of coffee. I got to thinking how Chambliss, unlike Waltz and Wilson, had heirs to his holdings if something untoward were to befall him. Maybe it's why he was still alive. "Great coffee this morning." Martha paused a second in hopeful anticipation then scampered back to the kitchen.

I enjoyed breakfast despite being haunted by what happened—or might have happened—with Diana Kilkenny. Martha returned twice to refill my cup.

I wrapped up breakfast and headed to the courthouse.

The clerk at the courthouse tried his best to be helpful. I suppose it wasn't every day that a real live Texas Ranger stopped by to examine property deeds and plats. I decided to focus initially on properties in the region surrounding Kilkenny's spread.

After a couple of hours of the clerk stumbling all over himself to be helpful, I came to realize that it took a special sort of person to love this sort of research. Some of it was fascinating, as the history of properties was revealed in the various documents. Some were downright boring.

It didn't take me long to locate the Chambliss place. His twenty thousand acres had been carved from a larger grant. Part of it bordered on the Kilkenny ranch. Then, it hit me. The Running Circle stood between the Bar K and the Guadalupe River. I slapped my forehead. Why hadn't I caught that sooner?

My mind raced with the possible tactics Diana might employ to get Chambliss to sell. Shucks, it might yet involve having Chambliss disposed of—and likely his wife, too. I felt the urge to track down Sheriff Vann, but knew I had more research. So long as I was here, it made sense to see whether other properties were vulnerable to Diana's intentions.

Another couple of hours of research paid off—sort of. Joseph Kilkenny himself had purchased a small five-thousand-acre spread seven years ago on the east side of Kerrville. It left me to wonder why he'd bought the large ranch just beyond the western boundary. I scratched my head.

"Problem, Mr. Ranger?" asked the clerk.

"Anything special about this property?" I pointed to the plat.

"Sets on the railroad," observed the clerk, pointing to

the cross-hatched line running the length of its border. "Owner reckons to build cattle pens."

I found myself beginning to think that Kilkenny was more deeply involved than I'd figured. It left me to wonder what he knew of his daughter's methods and whether he endorsed them?

"Can I help you any more, Mr. Ranger?"

I stood and prepared to leave. "Thanks for your help." I felt that my time at the courthouse had been quite worthwhile. I had uncovered a potentially ugly underbelly of intrigue in this small Texas town. It left me yearning to learn more of Kilkenny beyond his war stories and building a shipping business. I figured it was time to check in with Sheriff Vann.

It wasn't far from the courthouse to the jail. I walked Big Red up the street and hitched him out front of the jailhouse. I peeked in the window and saw Vann rifling through some paper, so I knocked and stepped inside.

The office reeked of coffee, sweat, and smoke. "How do, Sheriff?" I ventured.

Vann shook his head glumly and nodded toward the cells.

I shrugged and took a gander. They were empty. I turned back to Vann. "What the hell?!" I exclaimed.

"Somebody paid his bail. Garth Jones is supposed to show up for trial in two weeks. Meanwhile, he's free as a bird."

I felt my face flush with anger. The man who'd threatened to kill me was on the loose. I strove to keep myself under control. "Guess I'd better be watching my back," I intoned with hardcore irony.

"Sorry, Lucas. I sent a message to the hotel."

"Missed it. I've been at the courthouse doing some digging."

"Find anything?"

"Well, my day began with Sam Chambliss visiting me about Diana Kilkenny pushing on him to sell his Running Circle spread. At the courthouse, I found that his property lay between the Bar K and the Guadalupe."

Vann spat out a mouthful of coffee.

I ignored Vann, as he wiped coffee from his vest. "Kilkenny owns some property east of town along the railroad. Some fascinating coincidences are coming together." I let that sink in. "What do you know of Kilkenny's personal life? He has a daughter. Did something befall his wife?"

Vann shrugged.

"I'm curious as to whether the sheriff in Galveston County might know something?" I rubbed my chin thoughtfully.

"Have at it, Lucas. I'm just pleased that there haven't been any more killings."

"Yet," I said. "I'm heading to the telegraph office."

Vann began brewing a fresh pot of coffee.

I shook my head with just a bit of dismay and exited.

The telegraph office was at the railroad station. I checked the load in my Smith & Wesson, as I ambled up the street. With Jones out of jail, my senses were on high alert. Reaching the station, I began writing out a cryptic message.

Sheriff, Galveston County.

Seek background on Joseph Kilkenny.
  Wife? Children? Family? Associates?

. . .

Texas Ranger Lucas Dunn Jr.
  D Company, Frontier Battalion

Reply Kerrville, Texas

I watched the telegrapher send the message and asked that
any reply be delivered to my room at the hotel. It occurred
to me that I could have used the telephone, but I sought a
response on a piece of paper. There just seemed to be something more official about that.

    I reckoned that I'd head back to the hotel and await a
response. I'd barely reached the door of the telegraph office,
when the telegrapher told me to hold up. A message was
coming in. In but a couple of minutes, the telegrapher
handed me a response.

Texas Ranger Lucas Dunn Jr.
  D Company, Frontier Battalion

Joseph Kilkenny, Born 1841, Louisville,
Kentucky
    Farmer
    Quantrill Raiders, CSA 1860 to 1864
    Seaman 1864 to 1870
    Founded Kilkenny Freight & Shipping
1870
    Wife passed 1872

```
    Founded  Kilkenny  Parr  Land  Holdings
with Archer Parr 1886
    No children
    Moved Kerrville, Texas 1894


Henry Thomas
    Sheriff, Galveston, Texas
```

My eyes about popped from my head.

"You all right?" asked the telegrapher.

"Er, yes. I'm fine," I responded. "Just fine." The link to Archie Parr combined with Kilkenny having no children. I felt like a door had been opened toward solving the murders. "Damn!" I murmured and exited the station. Pieces of the puzzle seemed to be coming together. Still, I had only circumstantial evidence. Suspicions don't win court cases. What was Diana's connection to Kilkenny? How involved was Archie Parr?

SIXTEEN
BUSHWHACKED

MY MIND WAS ROILING AROUND with the possibilities spawned by this new information from the Galveston County sheriff. How careless of me. I walked past a ramshackle warehouse so dusty and rotting that a stiff wind might have blown it down. A sharp rock turned my ankle just enough to put me off balance. It caused me to bend over just as an explosion from a rifle rent the air asunder. A bullet whizzed past where my head had been. I dove into the dust while simultaneously freeing my Smith & Wesson. A second shot kicked dust beside my head. This was too close.

I crawled behind the wheel of a nearby wagon. It wasn't much protection. I heard a lever action, and another bullet came my way, splintering a wagon wheel spoke and sending shards past my ear. This bushwhacking was taking its toll. I was none too happy.

It didn't take but a moment to figure out my likely attacker. I laid low for a few moments more. Silence. I cautiously arose with the wagon between me and the direction of the gunfire. Scanning the street and surrounding buildings revealed nothing. Whoever shot at me had apparently run off. Were these near misses again with the purpose of scaring me off? If they were, the shooter had gotten far closer than previously.

With all my senses on alert I dusted myself off and headed for the saloon. My intuition told me that I just might find the shooter in a public place. I stepped into the Longhorn Saloon, let my eyes adjust to the dimly lit interior, and scanned the room. Garth Jones sat alone at a table beside the back wall. A half-full whiskey bottle sat before him next to an empty glass. This was my first clue that he might have been here a while. I turned to the barkeeper. "How long has he been here?"

"Couple hours. Ain't moved from the seat."

I thanked the barkeep and boldly strode over. Upon first glance, it appeared that Jones was unarmed.

Looking up at me through rheumy eyes, Jones snarled, "What do you want, you damned sonofabitch? Ain't it enough you put me in that godforsaken jail?"

"Somebody shot at me," I shared with an accusatory look.

Jones chuckled and belched. "I wouldn't have missed," he slurred.

I gauged him in his inebriated condition. It was obvious that Garth Jones had not tried to shoot me. Now, I faced the unsettling reality that an unknown assailant lurked somewhere around Kerrville and aimed to kill me. "Good luck, Garth."

"Luck got nothin' to do with it," he retorted.

I turned on my heels, dropped a dollar on the bar, and motioned the barkeep to keep serving Jones. I headed on out of the saloon. Now what? I was beginning to wonder whether there was anyone I could trust in this town.

What now? I needed to go off and think. First, I'd stop back at the hotel room.

As I passed the hotel desk clerk, he gave me a knowing sort of look. What could that have meant? I headed up the stairs. Reaching the top, a hunch gripped me. I sensed that I had a surprise visitor. My boots and spurs made enough noise to wake the dead, as I walked toward the door to my room. I halted just short of the door. I slipped the Smith & Wesson from my holster. I was about to reach for the door-knob when intuition made me pause. I heard a click followed by a boom as a shot blasted through the door. Another step, and I'd have been a dead man. A second shot boomed out.

I kicked open what remained of the door and stopped in gun first. The window was open, and curtains swayed in the breeze. I heard a thud outside, followed by hooves galloping away. I poked my head out the window but my assailant was nowhere to be seen. "Damn!" I cursed under my breath. Seconds later, Sheriff Vann came running up the stairs with gun drawn.

"What the hell?!" he exclaimed upon stepping over the debris and entering the room.

"That's two near misses in one day," I said, shaking my head.

"Something happened earlier?"

"You didn't hear the shots down near the warehouse?" I replied.

"I thought someone was shooting varmints. Sorry." Vann examined the door. "Do you think it could have been Jones?"

I gave an ironic laugh. "He was my first guess, too.

Jones is tying on a drunk over at the saloon. He couldn't hit the broad side of a barn." I shook my head with consternation. "Somebody figured I'm getting too close to solving the murders."

"Well, it's looking like you better solve it before the bushwhacker doesn't miss," advised Vann with a touch of ill-timed humor.

"I think I'll take a ride out to the Chambliss place."

Vann followed me down the stairs. As we stood on the walk out front of the hotel, he paused. "Say Lucas, did you hear from Galveston?"

"Yep," I answered cryptically.

"Helpful?" Vann pressed.

I sighed. Vann was insistent and I'd been sent to help him, so I owed a response to him. "Hard to figure. Sheriff Thomas said Kilkenny is a widower and had no children. He's also a partner in a land scheme with Archer Parr."

"Who the hell is Diana?" blurted Kilkenny.

I chuckled. "I reckon to find out."

Vann shook his head. "Damn, but this has taken a strange twist. You want company on your visit to Chambliss. I could watch your backtrail."

"More likely, you can ship my bushwhacked bones back to Nuecestown." I scanned the street, as there was no telling where the shooter lurked, if at all. "Thanks, Sheriff. I'll head out alone." Actually, my thinking was to seek out Chambliss later. Meanwhile, I was of a mind to do a bit of scouting on the Bar K.

Among the skills my dad and my old friend Buffalo Watts taught me were those entailing stealth and putting together the clues that ensured a successful hunt. I had ridden in a sweeping arc to the north of the Bar K and approached from the side opposite the main gate. I ground-hitched Tornado. He wouldn't stray far. I just reckoned to keep an eye on the main house for a couple of hours and observe any comings and goings.

I crawled to a vantage point overlooking the veranda behind the house. I could see the bench where Diana had done whatever she did to or with me. I hadn't been lying there long when Kilkenny walked into view. He was gesticulating wildly and talking angrily to someone. Fancy my surprise when Diana appeared. Oh, to have been close enough to overhear what was being said. Diana looked to be pleading about something.

I pulled out my binoculars to get a better look. I wasn't a lip reader, but something might be obvious. I focused in. Kilkenny was still ranting and Diana pleading. It was as though I were watching some sort of stage drama.

Imagine my amazement, when Diana grabbed Kilkenny and pushed him onto the bench. He continued to fuss, as she unfastened his belt. He spewed ever fewer words, as she opened his pants and pulled out his manhood. His expression quickly turned from anger to ecstasy. She finished and stood back with a satisfied look at Kilkenny's slumped form punctuated with a satisfied smile across his lips. She spit out his love juices, turned, and headed inside. Kilkenny finally sat up and shook his head dismayingly. He slowly arose and followed Diana into the house.

Whatever the relationship between the two, it seemed to verify that they weren't father and daughter. What was the nature of their relationship? It was surely spirited. Was she his mistress? What did she have to do with the land grabbing and the killings on the Guadalupe River?

I had been mulling over a way to trap whomever was behind the murders. It was time to visit Sam Chambliss and see whether he might be up for helping me out. I reckoned he would be the next target, given the critically important location of his Running Circle Ranch.

SEVENTEEN
SETTING THE TRAP?

I SCRAMBLED BACK TO TORNADO, feeling as though I needed to tell someone about what I'd just witnessed. It was a shame that horses didn't understand English, as I poured out what I'd seen and planned to do. I headed purposefully toward the Running Circle. I'd soon know how much sand Sam Chambliss had. Gnawing at me was just who the woman with Kilkenny truly was? I sought to shake it from my mind to no avail.

It didn't take all that long to find my way to Chambliss's spread. The Running Circle Ranch showed the wear and tear of the elements. Years of unrelenting assaults by the weather common to the hill country of central Texas had taken their toll. Little wonder that the aging Chambliss was unable to fully keep up. The prospect of Kilkenny's holdings surrounding him and pressuring him to sell must have seemed daunting.

I rode up cautiously to the Chambliss home. Gazing out to my left, I could see the Guadalupe lazily flowing by. "Sam! Sam Chambliss! You home?"

"Who's askin'?" came a female voice from inside.

"Texas Ranger Like Dunn here, ma'am. Met your husband the other day in Kerrville."

The door creaked open just a bit, and a head poked out. Creases of aging and gray hair gave testimony to the hard life of carving a life from the hills and prairies of this fast-disappearing final residue of the frontier. "I'm Amy Chambliss." A double-barrel shotgun preceded her stepping into the sunlight. I was grateful that it wasn't aimed at me, as I reckoned she knew how to use it. "Sam'll be back any minute. Jus' went to corral a maverick steer."

"Mind if I wait for him?" I made sure the sun caught my badge.

The suspicion in her eyes eased a bit. "Sure, Ranger Dunn. Step down an' set a spell." She caught me looking at the shotgun and put it shotgun aside. "Been Apache still lurkin' about an' other troubles. Care fer some coffee?"

I slid from Tornado's saddle. "Sure, Mrs. Chambliss. Coffee would be right fine." I parked my butt on a nearby bench.

Amy came out promptly with a cup of steaming coffee.

"Sam been gone long?" I asked.

She gave me a curious look. "Jus' a couple hours."

"Must be a steer with a mind of its own. I've had to deal with a few myself on my spread down Nuecestown way."

"You hitched?"

She didn't mean my horse. "Yes. Name's Cassie. We have a young'un and another on the way."

"Was yer pa…"

I noticed a change in her demeanor, as though something weighed heavily upon her. "Texas Ranger Captain Luke Dunn? Yes." I sensed that she was looking for help and assurance but was suspicious of everyone.

My answer seemed to raise my stock in her eyes. She took a deep breath. "Come. Come inside, Ranger Dunn," she said somberly and with what I felt was a feigned welcoming.

I thought her sudden hospitality a bit strange, but followed her in. I ducked low through the front door then stood, accustoming my eyes to the dim light. Lying on a bed lay a very pale-faced Sam Chambliss. Despite efforts to clean up, there was plenty of blood on the sheets around him. "My God, Sam, when did this happen? Where's the doc?"

Chambliss gave me a once-over through glazed eyes. He tried to speak, but the effort was too much.

"Horse brought him in a couple hours ago. Near fallin' from his saddle." She answered my question before I could ask. "Slug gone clean through. Blood everywhere."

I'd seen death before, and Chambliss was closing in on the Grim Reaper's scythe. It appeared as though the bush-whacker didn't always miss. "Sorry, Mrs. Chambliss."

She knew full well that Sam was done for. "Thirty year we been hitched," she lamented. "Good man."

"Did you call the doc?"

She faced reality head-on. "Ne'er git here in time. Sam's 'bout done, bless his soul." As she said the words, Chambliss' trembling hand reached for her but dropped limply as he breathed his last. She kissed his forehead and gently closed his eyes. Amy turned to me with tear-reddened eyes. "I'm gonna kill that Kilkenny bastard," she delivered with a deadly firmness that sent a chill up my spine.

"Let the law do its work, Mrs. Chambliss." The words sounded hollow off my tongue.

"Yuh done had months, Ranger. Now, they done took my man."

"Don't be doing something you'll be arrested for," I cautioned.

She laid a stone-cold look on me. "My life don't matter none."

My mind raced with what to do next. My plan to leverage Sam Chambliss's Running Circle to entrap whoever was scheming to grab land had just fallen apart. Amy Chambliss could mess up most any alternatives I might come up with. "You have sons, Mrs. Chambliss. Reach out to them. It's not right that they should lose their mother, too." I hoped I was reaching some inner part of her beyond revenge for Sam's murder. Would motherly instinct triumph? I reckoned it was the best I could come up with at the moment.

She sighed and sat gently on the edge of the bed, looking at her husband. "Could yuh help me bury him, Ranger?"

"Yes, ma'am. I can do that."

I spent the next hour digging a grave into which we reverently laid Samuel Chambliss to rest. I spoke a few words over the grave with hopes of sending his soul speedily to his Maker.

"Thanks kindly, Ranger." Her eyes penetrated mine. "Kin yuh promise me you'll bring the killer to justice, promise a good tight noose 'round his evil neck? I be holdin' off any revenge fer a time."

"Justice will be served, Mrs. Chambliss. I promise." I hoped and prayed I could deliver on that oath. An idea struck me like a bolt out of the blue. "Do you trust me, Mrs. Chambliss? Enough to do something bold?"

She'd not yet even had time to grieve her loss. "What yuh have in mind?"

"What if I let it be known that I was representing you in the sale of the Running Circle?"

"I ain't sellin' nothin'!" she blurted.

"I don't mean to sell it. Just use it as bait to trap the killer."

Amy studied my face. "Yuh look honest enough, Ranger. Yuh think it'll work?"

I shrugged. "Seems worth a try." I'd been working this case for nearly four months, and concocting an entrapment was affording me the first opportunity to deliver justice.

She stepped to me and gave me a hug. It was surely something she needed. "Don't be failin' me, Ranger." She gently pushed me away and knelt beside Sam's grave.

I mounted Tornado. I had to get the word out that I was representing the sale of the Running Circle Ranch. I reckoned a few words dropped at the hotel and saloon would quickly reach the appropriate ears. I smiled. Maybe this lame-brained scheme would actually work. I figured whoever was behind the murders would work with me, since they wouldn't be able to strong-arm Mrs. Chambliss into selling. Unlike those murdered on the Guadalupe, she had heirs. A sale—forced or legitimate—was the landgrabber's only alternative to gaining access to the river.

EIGHTEEN
LURING THE PREY

AFTER PUTTING the word out at the hotel, the saloon, and a couple of other places about town, I decided to catch up with Sheriff Vann. A spread of rain began to fall, so the main street began turning muddy in my brief jaunt from hotel to sheriff's office. I knew Vann disliked surprises, so I knocked.

"Come in," came the reply.

Entering, I came to an abrupt halt, as I tried to get a read on Vann. My eyes asked what the occasion was?

Vann was looking quite dapper with a stylish jacket and string tie. From what little I could see, he'd even polished his boots. "My wife's sister's getting married," he confessed. "Only wear this getup for special events, mostly funerals."

I smiled broadly and took a seat. "Sam Chambliss was bushwhacked out on the Running Circle range. I helped his wife bury him. There's no way Mrs. Chambliss can run that spread by herself, so she's reaching out to her sons for help. However, she's revenge-minded but will hold off. I promised her that I'd bring the killer to justice."

Vann shook his head. "Damn, Lucas! That's six! Time to solve this!" He was shaking with seething anger borne of frustration.

I ignored the sheriff's reaction. "Mrs. Chambliss and I worked out a plan. I'm pretending to represent her for the sale of the ranch. We'll see who comes forward."

"Hell, Lucas, I guess it's worth a try. Hope it doesn't get you killed."

"Oh, one more thing." I rubbed my chin as I measured my words. "I've got bad feelings about the Kilkenny woman. She's likely not even a Kilkenny. Leaves me to wondering who she is?"

Vann winced and forced a smile. "Some of the ladies about town have opinions."

"Bet they do," I enjoined, as I headed out the door. I led Tornado up the street toward the stable. I figured I'd sit a spell on a bench in front of the hotel and see what developed. I thought back to the advice Bass Reeves gave me about being patient and expecting the unexpected. I stabled Tornado and checked the load in my Smith & Wesson. I didn't think I'd need it, but any lawman worth his sand makes sure his weapons are in proper working order and ready when needed.

It was about mid-morning. I'd been sitting on the bench for about an hour, entertaining myself with thoughts of what Cassie might be up to back home. I caught a little shade from the overhanging roof. I could see hills stretching out in the distance beyond the town. It was like a little bit of heaven that called to strong folks to build a life. Why then, did folks try to steal it by illicit means? It caused me to wonder what drove folks like Joseph Kilkenny and Archer Parr? What made them happy? They seemed to seek their pleasures in things; objects, if you will. To my way of thinking that was a false happiness. For Parr, happiness seemed to be about prestige and the sort of popularity politicians sought. Kilkenny appeared to be driven by sexual pleasures and possessions. Both men sought power so as to exert influence. Then, there was Garth Jones. He was likely the only hell his mama ever raised. Jones was decidedly unhappy. Somewhere in his life, he'd lost any desire for happiness, if he ever had any to begin with. What of the woman? What of Diana Kilkenny—if that was her real name? From what I could tell, her happiness or more accurately, some level of euphoria was a concoction of using pleasure as a tool to attain influence over men. She sought power by any means necessary. The best word I could come up with to describe her was self-love. What was the over-arching connection among these folks? The choices they made entailed discernment; an ability to make good or bad choices. I reckoned I had taken a pretty good measure of Archer Parr and Garth Jones, but I was still trying to figure what drove the Kilkenny's? What drove them to come to Kerrville and rustle up trouble? Part of the answer to that likely involved Parr, but there had to be more.

Then, it hit me! I threw up my hands. Diana was Kilkenny's mistress. She was driven by her power over men, and the more powerful the men and greater the challenge to their succumbing to her wiles, the greater was her exhilaration, her ecstasy. By virtue of acquiring ever-more land, Kilkenny achieved greater power to influence the community, but more importantly to him, to hold sway over Diana. He even tolerated her dalliances with other men, knowing he had the ultimate hold on her. Perversely, I figured her throwing her charms around aroused him.

There I was, sitting on the hotel gallery with my mind floating off into the whatever, when a voice shook me from my musings.

"Lucas? Lucas Dunn?" came the insistent inquiry.

A woman's voice? I opened one eye and instantly shaded it from the sun. "Er...yes?"

"I hear that Amy Chambliss appointed you to sell her spread."

I lowered the brim of my hat to better shield my eyes. Diana Kilkenny?! I quickly gathered my thoughts. "That's true, Miss Kilkenny."

"Diana," she insisted. She was sitting on a fine saddle this morning on a gray filly.

"Sure. What you've heard is true, Diana."

Her eyes asked how I'd managed to wrangle that responsibility. She was likely cussing out the Chambliss's in the depths of her soul. "Guess you know we have interest in the Running Circle Ranch?"

I nodded while trying to contain a smirk. The fly had flown into my web. Now, I could sit back and enjoy her trying to manipulate me. She was outfitted in riding duds this morning. At that, her blouse and pants were so form-fitting as to leave little to the imagination. She sure could fill a saddle. Her hair formed a long braid down her back all the way to her waist. Her boots rose to just below her knees. I reminded myself that this was the woman throwing herself at me, leaving me a provocative note, and maybe hiring someone to bushwhack me. Wondering whether she had her way with me that night still gnawed mercilessly at me.

She must have known what I was thinking. "Amazing?" she threw out with a provocative smile. This was a woman who practiced what she preached. People were merely means to her ends. She suddenly grew serious. A gust of wind kicked up dust from the street and caused us both to shield our faces. "What's her price?"

"You get right to it, don't you, Diana?"

"Can we go someplace and discuss the matter? Your room?" Her lips spread fetchingly.

There was no way I'd find myself alone with this woman in a room that featured a bed. "There's a dining room inside. How about chatting over a cup of coffee." I reckoned to play her game but with my cards. The downside of succumbing to her manipulation was destruction... mine.

Diana dismounted, making sure I saw the curves of her rear end.

I couldn't help but appreciate her gentle curves, but I also noted the Winchester set in its scabbard hanging alongside her saddle. This was still a time when folks didn't generally venture out unarmed, as everything from rogue Indians to road bandits to rattlesnakes posed threats. I wondered how good she was with the rifle?

Hitching the filly, she led the way into the dining room. She paused at the stairway, as if to signal that we could still meet in my room.

I motioned to the dining room, and we took seats along the far wall. It was too early for midday meals, so we were alone for now.

Martha brought out two cups of steaming hot coffee. "Sugar?" she asked.

Diana nodded. She dropped a cube of sugar in her coffee and stirred thoughtfully.

"Can I get y'all anything?"

"Thanks, Martha. Not just yet." I gave her a smile that she properly read as Diana and me having business to conduct. "Just let me know," she offered, gave me a knowing wink, and made her way back to the kitchen.

I gave Diana a look that aimed to counter her seductive smile. "So, what's your real name and who is Joseph Kilkenny to you?" I wasn't mincing words.

She appeared momentarily flustered, as my question caught her totally off guard. "I thought we were discussing the sale of a ranch?" she persisted.

"I like to deal honestly with honest people." I took a sip of coffee. It was still hot enough to nearly burn my lips, but I kept a steady gaze on her. The silence blared.

"I think we're done here." She began to rise. I grabbed her elbow and yanked her solidly back onto her chair.

"No. We're not done," I said firmly. "Who are you?"

I could sense her brain burning, as she strove to decide her next move. "None of your business, you sonofabitch," she finally blurted. "Chambliss isn't selling the ranch, is he?"

"Sam Chambliss is dead. I represent his wife. And, you're right. She isn't selling. One of her sons is on his way here, as we speak."

Diana was stewing by now. Her attempt at using her female wiles had failed miserably, and it was clear to her that I'd figured out her convenient relationship to Joseph Kilkenny. She pushed back her chair out of my reach and scrambled for the door.

I let her go, having learned most of what I'd sought. She all but admitted that she wasn't a Kilkenny.

Martha appeared. "Susanna Wright," she stated flatly.

"Say what?" I asked.

"Sorry. I couldn't help but overhear. That's her real name. One of our Kerrville ladies found out yesterday." Martha smiled knowingly. "Susanna came from back east determined to make a name for herself. Hear tell she was one of those spoiled and bored little rich girls. An equestrian, she learned to be a trick rider and sharpshooter who tried out for Buffalo Bill Cody's Wild West Show. She busted an arm, so they wouldn't take her. Emotionally overwrought, she fell in love with a gambling man who turned out to be abusive and set her to prostitution. Joseph Kilkenny discovered the soiled dove in Galveston. He stole her away from the gambler, cleaned her up a bit, and set her to work entertaining himself and his business associates."

I whistled and smiled gratefully. "Thank you right kindly, Martha." I suddenly felt relaxed. "I think I will have a bite to eat."

"Special today is steak and potatoes with corn, gravy, and biscuits, Mr. Ranger." She gave a mischievous grin. "Course, that's the special every day."

"Sounds great." I sat back and mulled over my next move. If I was right, she'd up the ante of the game.

Thus far, six men had met their ends to serve Kilkenny's purposes. Susanna was merely his weapon of choice. Having noted the Winchester stored at her saddle, I began to wonder whether her involvement went beyond using her body. She was a woman dependent upon men to generate excitement, pleasure, and even entertainment to satisfy her personal tastes. Sharpshooter? How good was she with that Winchester? I dared not forget that she was all woman and harbored womanly instincts for better or worse.

Meanwhile, sharing with Sheriff Vann what I'd found out seemed to be in order, and I'd tend to that. I had an idea on how to trap Susanna, but I dearly wanted to nab Kilkenny. Perhaps his soul still held seeds of the rebellious guerrilla who rode with William Quantrill.

Having brought Vann up to date and shared my suspicions, I decided to ride out toward the Running Circle Ranch. The openness of the Texas hills and a crisp breeze in the air might spur a plan that worked and—importantly—didn't get me killed.

I pointed Tornado in the general direction of the Chambliss spread and gave him his head. As we plodded along, I took in the beauty of my surroundings. Cypress lined the banks of the Guadalupe River. My eyes roamed the cliffs along the south bank. Live oak and juniper were set among mountain laurel, sage grass, Indiangrass, and switchgrass. It was getting a tad late in the season for Indian paintbrush and bluebonnets, but a few lingered. Just enough to gild the lilies, so to speak. It was quiet. Frogs occasionally croaked and a few birds serenaded the world. While I yearned to be back at Heaven's Gate and the Cassie's waiting arms, these hills seemed a right-fine place to be.

There I was carelessly lost in my daydreams, when Tornado's ears perked up. He'd distinguished the click of a carbine's lever from the birds and frogs. My brain and body weren't ready to cooperate. A muzzle blast from a stand of live oak up high across the river tore the air asunder. I ducked low in my saddle too late, as a slug plowed its way up my lower left side and exited near my shoulder. Dear God, it hurt like blazes! The force was enough to separate me from the saddle, and I fell with enough force to knock most of the wind from me.

I lay there taking stock and trying to catch a breath. The slug had to have damaged some ribs as it drove its way through muscle and sinew. I lay still, as moving might draw a finishing shot. So far as my assailant knew, I was dead or headed to that end. I could feel the blood oozing from the entry and exit wounds, more so from the latter. I needed to plug the holes in my body, or I might bleed out. I stole a glance at the bluff and caught the glint of sunlight off a rifle barrel being pulled back. Whoever was up there must have figured I was dead and decided to leave.

I already felt myself weakening. The bullet must have done more damage than I realized. By my reckoning, it was at least five or maybe six miles to Kerrville. Tornado stood by. He'd flinched at the gunfire but recovered quickly. My hands were shaking. Could I get in my saddle and make it back to town? Face it, I wasn't going anywhere.

Between the bullet and the hard earth along the riverbank, my body ached. I struggled and managed to bring myself to a sitting position. It felt as though the slug had busted a couple of ribs on its path through my torso. I looked down at my left side. My shirt was staining red, red with my blood. I could only imagine how much blood was oozing from the exit wound in my shoulder. I desperately needed to stop the bleeding.

I managed to tear my bandana in two and press the pieces against the wounds. This wasn't going to be nearly enough. The entry wound was near my belt, so it was easier to exert enough pressure to staunch the bleeding there. I realized that the belt likely saved my life, as it altered the trajectory of the slug enough to avoid vital organs. I grabbed a stirrup and pulled myself up with great effort. The pain was excruciating. My head swam a little, and I leaned into Tornado to keep from falling. With my right hand, I was able to free my saddlebags and drop them on the ground. I fell more than slid to a seated position. A paroxysm of pain shot through me. I began rooting through my saddlebags to find something to stop the bleeding. I used my Bowie knife to cut a piece of leather and strapped it around my shoulder. I felt as though that at least temporarily stemmed the bleeding there.

Now, I needed to gather my wits. I needed to act before the wounds fully sapped my energy. Somehow, the wounds must be cleaned. I dragged my saddlebags with me, as I wormed my way down to the river's edge. Water from the Guadalupe was plentiful, but hot water would be best. I gathered some dry grasses and sticks to build a small fire. I placed a flat rock in the middle and waited for it to heat up. Once I had the fire going sufficiently, I scooped water in my tin cup and set it on the hot rock. I managed to unbutton my shirt and free my left side. From what I could see, the bullet had entered and exited cleanly. That was good but also bad. There was no bullet inside me, but there was also no telling what junk the bullet brought with it through the entry wound. Infection could ultimately spell the end of me. The fire was going pretty fair by now. I placed the blade of my Bowie knife amid the flames. I pulled some cotton wadding from my saddlebag. It was there thanks to my dad's urging so as to be prepared for times like I now faced.

Tentatively and with utmost care, I removed the dressing from the lower bullet wound. The water was near boiling as I dumped it over the wound. Oh my, but the scalding water was worse than the pain from being shot. The wound began to seep blood, so I grasped my Bowie knife and cauterized it, nearly passing out from the agonizing pain. Lady fortune had smiled upon me there on the bank of the river. I'd found some leaves of wooly lamb's ear, as I'd made my way to the river's edge. Buffalo Watts had told me how the Indians and mountain men used the leaves to draw infection from wounds. I plastered a leaf on the wound, placed a wad of cotton over it, and tied it down with a bandage strip around my waist.

Treating the entry wound took a great amount of my energy. I knew that I must deal with the exit wound. I couldn't see it, but knew it had to be the uglier of the two wounds. The treatment process had to be repeated but by feel. As I sat waiting to recover enough energy to tackle the exit wound, I was hit like double-struck lightning with an idea. If my bushwhacker thought I was dead, I ought to stay that way. It just might flesh the Kilkenny's out and cause them to do something stupid. I recalled hearing my dad talk about how power corrupts. The Kilkenny's were on the cusp of holding considerable power over the region. They'd surely make a mistake sooner or later.

Treating the exit would take the last of my strength. I lay back and fainted as much as fell asleep. I likely napped for a couple of hours, when a restless Tornado nudged me. There's nothing like the snout of a horse rubbing your cheek to bring you out of slumber. A snort in my ear pretty much brought me around. I took stock of my surroundings. My location could only be seen from the bluffs across the river, as I was sheltered from above the spot behind where I lay. A breeze stirred the highest limbs of the cypress. Crickets chirped, and a frog croaked. They could have cared less for the human lying grievously wounded on their territory. My ribs ached like no tomorrow, though the bullet wounds had calmed down. I snuck a peek under the poultice covering my lower wound. There was no inflammation. I assumed that was the case for the wound at my shoulder. Yer there was no salve for the throbbing pain in my shoulder and side. The good news so far as I could tell? I wasn't going to be the seventh victim on the Guadalupe. I watched a mountain lion amble down to the river's edge and take a long drink. They were right-graceful creatures, when they weren't looking to kill something for dinner.

By now, logic told me that the Kilkenny's were positioned to make a final offer to Amy Chambliss. I hoped she stayed strong, though it occurred to me that Susanna might not be above killing a woman. It occurred to me that while Garth Jones did some of the Kilkenny's dirty work, he was simply a dangerous foil. Given her marksmanship, Susanna apparently took care of the serious killing herself. Joseph

Kilkenny? Well, he simply enjoyed the fruits of her labors. I wondered whether she'd be bold enough to eliminate Amy Chambliss and her rancher son? That didn't make sense, as Amy still had her other son back east. I recalled her mentioning that he was studying law at the University of Pennsylvania in Philadelphia.

Other than suspicions and opinions, I still lacked hard evidence. I'd promised Amy Chambliss that I'd bring her husband's killer to justice. With Jones busy nursing an ongoing drunk, Susanna was my prime suspect. How deep was Kilkenny's yearning to get his hands on the Running Circle Ranch? I reckoned that he had quite purposely not gotten his hands dirty. Better to leave the nasty work to Susanna and her hirelings. He had a good thing going and was obviously reaping the benefits of her lascivious abilities. Why ruin it all by interjecting himself into the midst of it all?

I pulled some jerky from my saddlebags and made some coffee. I needed to maintain what little strength remained in my battered body. Another day of rest, maybe two, and I just might be able to climb up into my saddle and do some snooping. Was I kidding myself?

Shards of sunlight bounced from the bluffs across the river from me. I was still alive. Despite pain and weakness, I managed to swap the dressings on my wounds. I even made some coffee and finished the last of my venison jerky. The wound at my beltline didn't look too bad. There was no sign of infection. I could only guess at the condition of the wound on the back of my shoulder.

By now, folks in Kerrville would have counted me as

deceased. I dared not reveal to anyone that I remained among the living. I lamented that Cassie would eventually learn of my demise, yet laying low was a must. More immediately, Amy Chambliss's hopes might be crushed.

I decided to ride toward the Running Circle Ranch.

NINETEEN
BACK FROM THE DEAD

I NEEDED to take full advantage of my temporary status as dead. Back when I hunted with my father and the mountain man Buffalo Watts, they taught me the art of making snares. The simpler, the better, out in the wild country. The same approach ought to work here in Kerrville. Being a ghost might have its benefits.

It took some doing to climb into the saddle. Gratefully, Tornado was a patient cayuse. My left arm was pretty much useless, so I grabbed the saddle horn with my right and managed to generate enough momentum to swing into the saddle, releasing the saddle horn at the last second as my butt settled into the saddle. I sat there for a bit, catching my breath and gathering my wits. I feared that I'd start the wounds to bleeding, but far as I could tell, my dressings did their job. My head spun just a tad. I took a deep breath and waited for my brain to clear before heading Tornado up toward the trail north of the river. The Running Circle wasn't but a couple of miles off.

I approached Chambliss's spread cautiously, pulling up among a thick stand of junipers and with a clear view of the ranch house. There was a fancy carriage out front with a mighty fine gelding to pull the rig. A tall, lanky young man in a well-tailored suit was talking animatedly with Amy. I couldn't be certain, but I gathered from facial features that resembled Sam Chambliss that this was one of her sons. He didn't look like a rancher, so I reckoned he was a lawyer. The conversation looked heated. I saw what must have been her other son standing in the doorway. His arm was in a bloodied sling, and he looked a bit pale. Another bush-whacking victim? About this time, two riders moseyed into the picture. Danged if it wasn't Susanna Wright and Joseph Kilkenny. He was getting himself involved, after all.

I made out a word or two. The lawyerly son finally threw up his hands and shouted for the world to hear. "Just sell the damned place, ma!"

Amy pointed animatedly at Kilkenny and Susanna. If she'd had the shotgun in her hands, they'd have been dead right then and there.

What followed happened faster than hell could scorch a feather. The son in the doorway, began to lift the muzzle of the shotgun. I watched helplessly, as he struggled to cock the weapon but never quite got to aim it before the rifle across Susanna's saddle came into play, belching lead in a fiery explosion. A slug went square between the son's eyes. He was dead before he hit the ground. Amy began beating on her other son's chest. The air turned blue with her cussing.

Susanna took a bead on Amy. "Step away!" she shouted to the son.

With great pain, I managed to lift my Winchester from its scabbard. I was about fifty yards out. I levered a round, took careful aim on Susanna Wright, and was about to squeeze the trigger, when a shot rang out. Susanna went stiff in her saddle before slumping off onto the ground. She lay there writhing in pain. Kilkenny wasted not a second, as he turned and galloped off as fast as his horse could carry him.

Where had the shot come from? I heard a second horse galloping away.

To hell with playing dead. I spurred Tornado and dashed from my cover. We reined up in a cloud of dust. The surge had caused me enough pain to nearly make me black-out, but I managed to hold myself together. Amy and her son were aghast and standing stock still. In the excitement of the moment, I leaped from my saddle and knelt at Susanna's side. Her breathing was raspy. Blood spread in the dirt beneath her. She looked into my eyes. There was no flirtation in them, no alluring sexual pull. She was dying and knew it. I stroked her forehead and made her as comfortable as I could.

"Lucas," she murmured. "Lucas D-D-Dunn."

Frothy blood leaked from her mouth. Her lungs were about gone. "Amaz...we...we did not." She half smiled, closed her eyes, and breathed her final breath. Those final words might have been the first honest ones she'd spoken since coming under Kilkenny's spell. I gently laid her head to the earth and slowly, painfully, stood. I looked over at Amy Chambliss.

"Yer alive," I heard from Amy Chambliss. "Cord heah said yuh was dead." She motioned to the young man beside her. "Cord be my son."

I stood. Now, the pain clawed at me. My eyes locked onto the dressed-up dude standing helplessly beside the carriage. "Coward." That was all I could muster.

"Cord tole me to sell to Kilkenny." Amy was torn apart with grief and anger. Her world had come down around her just because a power-hungry bully wanted access to the river. Her son lay dead in the doorway to her home, and her husband was buried out back. Her turncoat son sought to have her sell out to Kilkenny. What an utter mess!

"What kind of son are you?" The venom in my eyes must have penetrated to young Cord's soul.

Young Chambliss looked around desperately for an escape. His mother grabbed his arm and spun him to face her. "Yuh heard the man! Ansuh the question!"

Cord collapsed against the carriage. "I...I'm sorry, ma," he finally blurted.

Amy looked over at me and then down at Susanna. "Bitch kilt my man an' my son," she lamented coldly.

I was still wondering where the shot that killed Susanna had come from. "I'm sorry, Mrs. Chambliss."

She finally really looked at me. A hint of blood had seeped from my shoulder wound. "Dang, Ranger. Yuv bin shot!"

"I'm on the mend. She thought she'd killed me." I nodded toward Susanna's body. I needed to catch up with Kilkenny, but the mystery of who had killed Susanna lingered with me. "Folks in Kerrville think I'm dead. I want to keep it that way for now." I turned to her son. "Cord, do you think you can stay here and care for your mother until I get things wrapped up? I can't have you siding with that rascal Kilkenny."

Cord took a deep breath and looked at his mother. "I'm sorry, ma. I'll stay." He looked me in the eye and then down at Susanna. "You'd be right to figure that she worked her wiles with me." He shook his head and went to care for his brother. He glanced at Susanna's inert form. "I'll deal with her later."

Given my wounds, there was no way I'd be any help burying Amy's son. Watching Cord and his reactions gave me a squirrelly feeling. Something didn't seem quite right. Maybe it was the cold, calculating manner I'd seen lawyers take on. How had he known I was dead? Why was he advising his mother to sell? Did he have a connection to Kilkenny? There were too many unanswered questions. "I've got to head to Kerrville, Mrs. Chambliss. Hopefully, I won't be long." With great effort, I climbed into Tornado's saddle. I winced, but held myself together. I still had to figure how to get to Vann's office sight unseen. I headed off, though my feelings about Cord Chambliss were working on me.

I desperately needed to rest. I was also starving and had dared not ask the grieving Amy Chambliss for food.

TWENTY
UNEXPECTED TWISTS

I DIDN'T MAKE it but a couple of miles before my head began to swim. The exertion of riding was simply too much for my body. Making it to Kerrville wasn't yet in the cards for me, and dark clouds were looming on the horizon. Last thing I needed was a rainstorm. Tornado seemed to sense my distress and slowed to a walk, as my eyes searched for shelter. I found an overhang near the river under which I could rest and be protected from the elements. Dropping my saddlebags and bedroll, I slipped from my saddle. I managed to free my Winchester from its scabbard. I didn't have the energy to unsaddle Tornado. Best I could do was ground hitch him where he stood.

I did what I could to inspect my wounds. There was a bit of seepage from the dressings and the skin up my left side had turned a deep purple. I'd counted on reaching Kerrville and finding some grub. Hunger began to gnaw at me. Worse, I felt a tad feverish. Finding a doctor was in order, but I wasn't going anywhere just yet.

I spread my bedroll and lay back figuring to rest a bit before continuing to town. Maybe a nap would revive me.

My mind roiled with putting together the intricate puzzle pieces Kilkenny and his cohorts had created. Had Garth Jones gotten sober enough to shoot Susanna Wright? I felt my eyelids grow heavy and was soon sleeping soundly.

My equine alarm clock nuzzled me just as the sun crested the horizon the next morning. My mind felt refreshed, but my body didn't want to cooperate. I lay there. Bass Reeves had advised me to be patient, but I didn't think that had anything to do with recovering from a gunshot wound.

I had no idea what day it was. I assumed that I'd slept one night but could not be certain. I was surprised that some passerby hadn't spotted Tornado, as he wasn't hidden from sight like I was. It had rained briefly which might have discouraged some from venturing out. I struggled mightily and managed to sit up. I watched the Guadalupe flowing past and heard raindrops dropping from cypress limbs. Now and again, a frog would croak, and birds would sing. Other than that, all was at peace—except what was in my head.

Somehow, I had to get up and find my way to Vann's office. I looked upstream, and my heart froze. Not fifty feet away, a pair of yellow eyes were sizing me up. Mountain lion! I followed its lithe body to the tip of its twitching tail. Tornado's eyes were wide, nostrils flared, ears up. My Winchester ever-so-cautiously found its way into my hands from beside my bedroll. My left arm was barely functional enough to support the stock. I levered a round into the chamber. The click spooked the big cat, and he lit out at a run. I relaxed. I hadn't wanted to kill the beast, but had no qualms about defending myself and my horse.

The incident served to inject newfound energy into me. It was enough to motivate me to stand. Just maybe I could make it to Sheriff Vann. The movement with the rifle had taken the starch from my left arm, so I slowly gathered my saddlebags and bedroll with my right hand. Frustration was a word inadequate to my situation. I slipped the Winchester into the saddle scabbard, took a deep breath, and managed to mount Tornado. It's amazing how animals can sense when their human is struggling. Tornado could be a ball of energy in a fight, but now he was gentle as a lamb.

I reminded myself that I was dead, as I traveled off the road leading into Kerrville. I reckoned to stealthily sneak up behind Vann's office and enter through the back door. A light rain began falling, and I reckoned that might discourage folks from venturing out unless they absolutely had to. It took nigh unto three hours to make my way a mere five miles. I'd managed to wrestle my slicker from behind my saddle, as the rain began picking up intensity.

At last, I found myself behind the jail. Far as I could tell, no one had seen me. Far as everyone but Amy Chambliss and her son knew, I was dead. The thought tore at me in the sense that Cassie and my folks would likely receive the news and be morning. Cassie would be a widow with a young child and another on the way. She'd fear Sean growing up without a father. There was more to my fears, but I couldn't deal with them at the moment.

I hitched Tornado and made my way to the back door of the jail. It was locked. I knocked. No sound from within. I pulled out my revolver and rapped louder on the door. Finally, there was a stirring inside. I heard footsteps.

"Hang on, dammit! We got a front door, yuh know!" The steps stopped. "Who goes?" came a question out of an abundance of caution.

"Lucas Dunn," I replied weakly.

The door swung open. "Damn, you look like hell!" exclaimed Vann.

I stumbled inside.

Vann grabbed me before I could fall. Naturally, he grabbed my wounded side, causing me to nearly faint with the intense pain. He swung open a cell door and sat me on a cot. "I'll fetch the doc," he said with a look at my bloodied shirt and pale features before heading out the door.

"Damn, son. You're lucky to be alive," assured the doctor. "Those poultices likely saved your life. Infection would surely have ended it all for you."

Vann simply looked on anxiously awaiting the opportunity to ask what happened.

"You'd best be resting for a few days, son," advised the doctor.

I smiled. No gunshot wounds were going to stop me from finishing what I'd set out to do. I lay back after the doctor finished tending to my wounds.

The doc stood to depart.

"Doc, you must promise to not tell a soul that I'm here. So far as anyone is concerned, I was shot and killed. Promise?"

He smiled and nodded then turned to Vann. "I'll send you the bill, Sheriff."

Vann saw the doctor out and returned to me. "Tell me what happened?" he asked while pulling up a chair. "Oh, and I stabled your horse out back beside mine. I threw a blanket over him. Damned hard to hide an Appaloosa."

I laid the whole story out for him, including my suspicions about Cord Chambliss and Garth Jones. "I'm not sure what Cord's connection was with Kilkenny, though he might have hooked up with Susanna back when she was in Philadelphia. That'd be a big coincidence but possible. As to the shooter, I see Garth Jones is still out and about," I said with a scan of the empty jail cells. I didn't mention Susanna's final words assuring me that she hadn't had her way with me that night on the veranda.

"You have a plan, Lucas?" asked Vann.

"Well, Kilkenny thinks Susanna killed me, and Jones likely eased his own conscience by killing Susanna and also thinks I'm dead. My only worry is the Chambliss boy. If he's tied in with Kilkenny, he'll warn him that I'm still alive. Right now, I suspect Cord's mother has him staying close, but he'll surely wrangle himself free of her."

"You're not in any condition to do much," observed Vann. "And as to me arresting Kilkenny, I only have hearsay."

"I'm tougher than I look, Sheriff," I assured Vann. "One way or another, I'm heading out to the Bar K and confronting Kilkenny. The mere sight of me just might cause him to come clean." As I said the words, an idea came to me. "I'm going to need you to come with me to the Bar K as a witness tonight. With a full moon and starlit sky, the setting will be dang nigh perfect."

"What do you have in mind?" queried Vann.

I chuckled even though it sent a jolt of pain through my left side. "You're looking at a ghost." I rubbed my chin thoughtfully. "Find me a white sheet and white hat, Sheriff."

Vann nodded and gave a knowing smile as he began to catch on to my game.

Long about midnight, I slowly and painfully raised my body from the cell bunk. It was strangely silent. Vann was supposed to wake me and be ready for our adventure. I looked up the hallway in the direction of the sheriff's office and saw his inert form lying face down. There was no blood, and he was breathing. I went to open the cell door, but it was locked. Frustrated, I had no choice but to sit and wait for Vann to come to. Somebody was on to me, but who?

I laid back on the cot. Patience advised Bass Reeves. Ha! Patience was a living hell.

Finally, a groan emanated from the hallway. I turned to see a decidedly groggy Vann rise to his knees. His hand went to the back of his head, but he pulled it away upon hitting the spot where he'd been struck. He looked up in my direction. "Damn!" was all he could say.

"Any idea who hit you?" I asked.

It was quite clear that Vann was angry. He'd apparently let his guard down. "Jones! Sonofabitch came here last night and caught me when I turned away for just a second."

It was still dark out, but Vann had been unconscious for at least four hours. Whatever Jones was up to, he had plenty of time to do it. "What's Jones hoping to do?" I mused aloud. "Well, maybe it's not too late," I suggested.

Vann shook his head. "Really?"

"Nuts, Sheriff. I'm sitting here with a couple of bullet holes in me and you've got a bump on your noggin. Where's your fighting spirit?"

"Damn Texas Rangers," he spouted resignedly. "Let me get my shotgun," he added while staggering to the gun rack.

That was more like it. I gathered up the sheet and swapped my hat for the white one Vann had found for me.

★★

With Garth Jones knowing I was alive and us being clueless as to what he was up to, we knew our chances of success were seriously diminished. Nevertheless, I was bullheadedly determined to entrap Kilkenny.

Vann and I would have been a sight to behold for anyone awake and about at two o'clock in the morning. Two semi-conscious lawmen stumbled their way to their horses and headed to the Bar K. With any luck, we'd arrive just before sunrise. Reality was setting in. Was Jones hiding somewhere and fixing to bushwhack us. Where was Cord Chambliss? Was Kilkenny even at home?

The sun was still well below the horizon, but dawn was creeping up as we passed through the Bar K gate. We cautiously made our way toward Kilkenny's house. The house soon came into view. We reined in at the sight before us.

"Damn!" I murmured.

Cord Chambliss's carriage sat in front of Kilkenny's house. Yep, there it was. What was Amy's son up to?

"I'm still figuring to go around back and lure Kilkenny out onto the veranda," I whispered to Vann. "That Cord fellow is a coward. He'll do nothing." I took as deep a breath as I dared and dismounted. The pain caused me to pause.

"You up to this, Lucas?" asked Vann.

I winced. "No choice, Sheriff." I grabbed the sheet.

Vann followed me around toward the iron gate at the back entrance to the veranda. Anyone observing us would have had a good belly laugh. We finally arrived at the gate. It was imposing but the lock was not.

"Got the shears?" I asked.

Vann looked at my left side and my weakened arm. "Better let me do this," he whispered and promptly snipped the lock loose. A kerosene lantern hung just outside the entrance. I freed it from its hook and slipped inside. "You keep an eye out and that peashooter in your holster handy in case of trouble." I swallowed hard and wrapped the sheet over me. I bent over as best I could and splashed some white dust from the ground over my face to give me a more ghostly appearance. In the dim light, I reckoned that I had to look like an apparition come back from the dead. It was time. I lit the lantern and held it aloft as best I could. I mustered my deepest, scariest voice. "Joseph Kilkenny," I howled. Nothing. "Joseph Kilkenny...murderer...thief." I was delivering my ghostly pronouncements as scarily as I could. "Joseph Kilkenny."

Finally, Kilkenny emerged. Shock rather than fear was writ large on his face. "Who? What?" he ventured in a worrisome tone. Then, he realized who the ghostly creature was. "You...you're dead!" he exclaimed. "I didn't do anything! It was that woman! I just wanted the land!" Sometimes an overly-quick denial of wrongdoing is an admission of guilt. He'd just thrown Susanna under the wagon and run her over.

I expect it would have been asking too much for it to be just Kilkenny and me facing off. The spineless, weak-kneed, yellow-bellied Cord Chambliss stepped behind Kilkenny and stuck his skinny maw out from behind. Kilkenny became his human shield. "Him! I saw him alive! He's no ghost!" he declared loud enough to wake the dead.

Kilkenny was momentarily flustered. Bumbling syco-phantic Cord Chambliss had become the wild card in the deck. "That you, Lucas?!" asked Kilkenny nervously.

I'd surprised Kilkenny enough for him to have acknowl-edged some personal role and known of Susanna's part in his charade. He and Chambliss were unarmed. Neverthe-less, I cautiously placed the lantern on the ground and dropped the sheet. I unholstered my Smith & Wesson revolver. "You're under arrest for accessory to murder, Joseph Kilkenny." I motioned Vann to come in. "Sheriff Vann here has witnessed your confession."

Cord Chambliss made a move to run, but stumbled to his knees.

"You stay where you are, Cord Chambliss. I'm not sure how you're involved, but your mother's going to be your judge and deliver sentence on you." I turned to Vann. "You want the honor of cuffing him?" I dared not forget that, while Kilkenny was elderly, he'd ridden with Quantrill and sailed the seas. There was no telling what he might try.

Vann stepped forward and cuffed Kilkenny just to be on the safe side.

"Let's go...you and young Chambliss here take a ride to Kerrville. We can have a little talk at the jail." I was about to help Vann herd the two to the stable when we all heard the lever of a rifle. "Down!" I hollered.

The bullet nipped Cord's ear. He'd ducked too slowly. The rest of us were eating dirt, as a second bullet whizzed past. I reckoned it had to be Garth Jones. From the lack of accuracy, he was either too far off to aim accurately or had done some more drinking. It could have been both.

"Come on!" I yelled. "Get inside!" It didn't take but another couple of seconds to dive into the house. It was enough time for two more shots to sing their song through the early morning air. I actually smiled at the thought of Jones losing his touch. He'd been right on target with Susanna Wright and who knows who else before. I had to be grateful that he was losing his touch.

I couldn't worry about Jones for now. Even if he'd been drinking, I figured him to have enough smarts to not attack us inside Kilkenny's house. No self-respecting gun-for-hire would do something so stupid. We ran down the hallway and stopped at the foyer. Where was Garth Jones lurking?

Dare we venture out? Then again, maybe he, as they say, lit a shuck and decided to await another opportunity to work his brand of evil.

There we were—a mostly functioning Texas Ranger, a capable local sheriff, an ego-centric power-hungry crook, and a cowardly sniveling lawyer nursing a wounded ear— all standing breathlessly in the foyer. All eyes turned to me, and I was determined to get Kilkenny to the jail.

"I'm thinking whoever's trying to bushwhack us isn't going to hang around waiting for us." My words were more hope than fact. I knew that Tornado and Vann's horse were over near the barn. If we were to get to Kerrville, we had to saddle up mounts for Kilkenny and Chambliss.

"You're going to get us killed," insisted Kilkenny.

I laid a smile on Kilkenny. Throwing caution to the wind, I stepped out the front door and scanned the area. Young Chambliss's carriage stood out front. The sun was just about to break above the eastern hills. All was silent save for a cock crowing out there somewhere. This was going to be a bold test of what I was made of. Did I have enough of my legendary father's blood in me to venture out? Sweat appeared on my forehead, mixing with the white dust I'd sprinkled on myself to appear ghostlike. Shucks, the ghost ruse had worked—sort of. My still-healing shoulder wound throbbed a bit. I took as deep a breath as my sore ribs allowed. With nary a word, I headed for the carriage. I reckoned to use it as a shield.

I stood at the carriage and listened. No round was being chambered that I could hear. The cock crowed again. I waved at Vann to bring Kilkenny and Chambliss to join me at the carriage, and the four of us headed for the barn.

TWENTY-ONE
INCONVENIENT TRUTHS

KILKENNY SAT IN HIS CELL, a rueful expression
pasted across his face.

We really had nothing to charge young Chambliss with
but put his sorry butt in a cell anyway. He was beginning to
get his lawyerly hackles up, and I was quick to dissuade
him of that tactic.

It was time to tie up loose ends. Vann and I stood in his
office just out of earshot of our two jail residents. "We have
enough on Kilkenny to send him to Huntsville, John."

Vann gave me a knowing nod of agreement. "Think we
can get him to admit to the entire scheme?"

"I doubt we can indict him for murder, though he's all
but admitted enough to be charged as an accessory. We
didn't find anything unlawful with his land acquisitions. As
to Archer Parr, he seems to be clean. He'll be a force to be
reckoned with one of these days—politically, that is."

"You want to do the questioning, Lucas?" Vann was
giving me the privilege as a sort of back-handed acknowledgment of my having collared Kilkenny.

"Well, no time like the present to get started," I said and turned toward the row of cells. My strategy was to begin with young Chambliss. He was a tad scared. Being wounded by a bullet and then being incarcerated will tend to do that. He was conflicted between his legal schooling, whatever relationship he might have had with Susanna Wright, impact of his association with Kilkenny, and the bullwhip his mother would surely like to lay onto him. I let Vann unlock Chambliss's cell door.

"How's that ear feeling, Cord?"

Chambliss's hand reflexively went to the dressing we'd applied to his ear.

"Guess your mother's likely wondering where you are," I stated matter-of-factly.

Chambliss tried to gather himself. "You charging me with something?"

I looked over my shoulder at Kilkenny, sitting mournfully in the next cell. "Depends," I said.

Chambliss flashed me a questioning look.

"What's your connection with Mr. Kilkenny here?"

Chambliss sighed resignedly. "I had a brief liaison with Miss Wright back in Philadelphia a couple of years back. I say brief, because she left Philadelphia the day after we... we...you know." He ventured a glance at Kilkenny. "Guess she wound up in Galveston and connected with Kilkenny. When he showed an interest in my family's property, she must have recalled the tumble she'd had with me. When my father was murdered, she worked her persuasive ways with me to lure me back here to Kerrville and get my mother to sell to Kilkenny."

"And?" I asked.

"You've likely seen her in action," Chambliss replied.

I tried to imagine Susanna working her female wiles on the gangly lawyer and tried to shake the image from my mind's eye. Her voluptuous, gorgeous body connecting with... I shook it off.

"Did Miss Wright speak of her relationship with Mr. Kilkenny?" I reckoned to get to why we had Cord sitting here in a jail cell. Material witness? Maybe. He seemed desperate to get away from the Kerrville jail.

Chambliss laid a fleeting look on Kilkenny. "Miss Wright didn't say much about Kilkenny here. She knew that she couldn't play the father-daughter role due to our previous acquaintance. She visited me at the hotel and had her way with me." He paused as though turned on by the vividness of the memory. "I didn't resist. She was damned good."

I could understand Cord's failure of the flesh, but chiseling his mother was beyond the pale. "So, you fell for her game?" I pressed.

"Ma wasn't going to be able to care for the place herself, and my brother had his own spread. I thought she should get whatever money she could for the Running Circle."

The way Cord spoke, he likely would have advised her without Susanna's urgings. "What about your brother?" I asked.

"When Susanna shot him, I was shocked. I admit that my knees went weak, unaccustomed as I am to violence. I reacted poorly."

I felt true contrition begin to emerge. "Are you saying that Susanna was working for Kilkenny? Did he know of her murderous rampage?"

Cord Chambliss began to weep. "Sh-sh-she told me I'd be a dead man," he sniveled, "if I didn't help Kilkenny get the Running Circle."

I stole a glance over my shoulder at Kilkenny. He was in a fuming rage but silent. "Did she hire Garth Jones?"

"Don't know."

I reckoned young Chambliss was telling the truth. I exchanged a look with Vann. He nodded. "We're going to release you, Cord. Stick around Kerrville for a couple of days while we sort things out. Not sure you can mend your ways with your mother, but motherhood is a tough bond to break."

Vann swung the cell door wide open, and Chambliss wasted no effort in exiting. "Er...thanks," he murmured with barely a backward eye to Kilkenny.

I caught Vann's eyes. Now, the real work was about to begin.

Vann unlocked Kilkenny's cell, and we strode in.

I gave Kilkenny a hard look. Not an ounce of remorse was evident. "You going to make it easier on yourself and confess?" I didn't have to mention the alternative.

Kilkenny sat close-mouthed.

"Wish I had my dad's old friend, One Arrow, with us, Sheriff. He was a Comanche warrior who knew how to get the truth out of folks right quickly." I rubbed my hands in feigned glee. "It got messy, but sure was effective."

Kilkenny's face said I wouldn't dare.

"What do you think, Sheriff? Maybe just a little?" My implication was plenty clear.

Vann immediately caught on. "The jail is pretty much closed up tight, Lucas. Screams shouldn't carry." He was fully enjoying my strategy.

Panic began to set in with Kilkenny.

"You have a towel to mop up the blood?" I asked Vann.

He promptly fetched a large towel. "This do?"

I nodded and slipped my Bowie knife from its scabbard. I waved it around easy-like and tested its edge for sharpness. "I expect Mr. Kilkenny here has some recollections of his time with Quantrill's Raiders, maybe even fighting off pirates on the high seas."

Kilkenny's wrists were still handcuffed behind his back. He sought footing as he began to try to shrink away from me, but there was nowhere for him to go.

"Can you hold him down, Sheriff?"

Now Kilkenny was in full panic. His eyeballs were nearly popping from his head.

"The Comanche used to like to cut off a victim's *cajónes* and stuff them in their mouths. I'm not thinking of going quite that far." I winked at Vann. "Let's begin with fingernails."

Vann turned Kilkenny onto his stomach.

I grabbed a finger and stuck the point of the Bowie knife blade into the tip just enough to draw pain and blood.

"Noooooooo! Nooooooo! I'll talk!" screamed Kilkenny.

Vann flipped him on the cot, so the vile creature was facing me.

"You cut me, you damned Texas Ranger! Ain't legal!" he growled.

"He hasn't learned, Sheriff. Flip him back over, and I'll do another finger." I tested the edge of the Bowie knife again but inches from Kilkenny's face.

"No! I'll tell you what you want to know, damn your hides."

"You ready to write this down, Sheriff?"

Kilkenny went on to spill the beans, casting most of the most heinous deeds on Susanna Wright and taking pains to leave Archer Parr out of the scheming. Garth Jones was hired by Susanna to do some of the dirty work, but Kilkenny couldn't or wouldn't say specifically whether he killed anyone other than Susanna.

"Do you know who shot those first two ne'er-do-wells?" I pressed.

Kilkenny stole a glance at my still-unsheathed Bowie knife and gave my question some deep thought. "One of her flings. I think his name was John White. Never met him, but she said he gambled and sported a Derringer."

That fit with what we knew, so I was inclined to believe that Kilkenny was being truthful. "Miss Wright was quite a cut-throat vixen," I observed.

"And damned good in bed—or pretty much anywhere," offered Kilkenny as though fondly reminiscing.

"All this to acquire land?" I pondered aloud.

Kilkenny nodded ruefully.

Vann stepped forward. "Sign this, Mr. Kilkenny."

Kilkenny read the transcript and put his signature to it. He wasn't facing murder, and while his purposes had been dreadful, a good lawyer would get him a light sentence at the prison in Huntsville.

"If I could trouble you, Ranger Dunn?"

I faced him.

"If you could be kind enough to bring me a book or two from my library?" There was still no contrition. No apology for all the evils he'd wreaked upon Kerrville. I shook my head and followed Vann up the hall.

"I must get to a phone, Sheriff."

"There's one in the hotel, Lucas."

Off I went. Cassie needed to know that I was alive and well.

TWENTY-TWO
FUGITIVE ON THE RUN

THE TELEPHONE RANG. After what seemed like far too long, someone picked up the earpiece. "Yes?" came a gravely voice. I recognized it as Pastor Dixon.

Is Cassie home?"

Silence.

"This is Lucas. Is she home?"

"What sort of sick, demented person are you?" challenged Dixon.

"It's me. I'm alive." I insisted. I overheard muffled talking.

A cracking, barely-audible female voice spoke into the telephone. "Who is this?"

"Mother? It's me, Lucas."

"Oh, Lordy!" she screamed. "Cassie! Cassie! It's Lucas! He's alive!

There was a fumbling of the telephone. "Lucas?"

"Oh dear God, it's great to hear your voice, sweetheart. Yes, it's me. I'm very alive." I wasn't ready to tell her that I'd nearly been killed.

"Where are you?" Her words nearly burst from her.

"I'm in Kerrville and will head home. I solved the case."

There was silence.

"I miss you."

"I love you, too, Lucas." She broke down, sobbing with relief.

"Let's talk tomorrow, Junior." It was my mother.

We hung up.

As anxious as I was to be headed home, my wounds had caught up with me. My ribs and the muscles up my left side ached. The bullet wounds had only begun to heal. I slowly headed up the stairs to my room. Upon reaching the landing, I was able to see something pinned to the door of my room. A crudely-drawn Texas Ranger badge was sketched on the envelope. Sighing, I opened it and pulled out a slip of paper. The words were about as dreadful as any man could imagine. "I KNOW WHERE YOU LIVE." It had to be Garth Jones's doing. It was his handwriting.

I put my right arm against the doorjamb and leaned my forehead into it. "Why, Lord? Why?" I asked. Would this case give me no peace? What sort of depraved animal was Garth Jones?

Jones had a pretty fair head start on me. There I was, bone tired and half asleep on my feet. I was in no shape to travel. Determined, I pushed through the door and began to stagger about gathering my belongings.

I awoke on the floor of my room with a late afternoon sun casting golden shafts through the window. I shook off cobwebs and looked about. My side felt like it'd been kicked by a mule. I must have bent over to retrieve something and toppled in a heap. My brain told my body to get up, but the past few days since being shot had finally caught up to me. So far, I'd managed to sit up. With my right hand, I grasped the bedpost and slowly pulled myself up to the edge of the bed. I was not exactly the six-foot-three, well-muscled young Texas Ranger that some dime-store novelist might glorify as impervious to bullets. I'd only been shot once before when I'd been on the vigilante case, but this was far rougher to deal with.

I saw the note from Garth Jones lying on the floor. I desperately needed to get home. No time to wash or shave. Gathering my belongings and staggering down the stairs, my only thoughts were of heading for home to protect Cassie.

The livery stable loomed ahead. I threw the stable boy two bits and had him saddle Tornado. To his credit, the young man cast a concerned look my way. I was grateful that he was there to help me into the saddle. I ignored his caution about traveling at night.

As I nudged Tornado from the stable, a single gunshot exploded from up the street near the jail. I slumped in my saddle. Duty called.

I heard hooves galloping away, then saw Sheriff Vann on a dead run to the jail. I urged Tornado to a canter, though it hurt like all blazes. I arrived at the jail in time to meet Vann as he emerged from having investigated whatever had happened. I gave him a questioning look.

"Kilkenny's dead," said Vann angrily.

In a perverse sort of way, I was relieved. Garth Jones had surely done the shooting, and that meant he hadn't headed to Nuecestown yet. "Sorry, Sheriff," was all I could muster in my less-than-full-witted condition.

Vann sighed resignedly. "Not your fault, Lucas. I just left for a minute to get some grub, and now this. Likely that Jones fellow, and he's long gone. Tying up his loose ends, I reckon." It was obvious that he didn't have the inclination to gather a posse to pursue Jones. "Damn good riddance," he blurted. He shook his head and then looked up at me slouched in Tornado's saddle. "Where the hell you going?"

"I've got to get home. There's a problem I must deal with." I didn't feel it was fair to burden him with my problem, given the clean-up he now faced. With the murders solved, he was faced with getting Kerrville settled down. Folks needed to feel safe again. "I'm sure Jones is headed far from Kerrville," I assured him. I didn't figure to tell him that I knew exactly where Jones was headed.

The sheriff cocked his head and put a couple of fingers to the brim of his hat as a respectful goodbye gesture. "I'll be sure to let Captain Hughes know what a fine job you did. I'm personally much obliged." He took an apprising look at me astride Tornado. "You ride gentle, you hear." Then, he smiled. "You make a helluva ghost, Dunn." The smile disappeared, and he went back to take care of Kilkenny's body.

I headed for the telegraph office. I wasn't about to dismount, so rapped on the office window. The clerk smiled and nodded sort of knowingly at my condition. He handed me a paper and pen. I scribbled the message and handed it back to him. He raised his eyebrows and quickly went to work.

SHERIFF JOHN MCTIERNAN
NUECES COUNTY, TEXAS

SHERIFF: FUGITIVE GARTH JONES HEADING TO NUECESTOWN. THREAT
TO HEAVEN'S GATE RANCH. ON MY WAY TO HELP.

TEXAS RANGER LUCAS DUNN, JUNIOR

COMPANY D, FRONTIER BATTALION

After receiving the clerk's nod that the message had been received, I headed Tornado eastward into a darkening landscape. I'd at least have warned Cassie.

Jones had a pretty fair lead on me, and I was in no condition to make this a horse race. I had to stay alert, as there was still a chance that he might try to bushwhack me. I judged Jones to be an experienced hired gun, but felt confident that even in my diminished condition, I had a better set of the skills required to handle the hills of central Texas. Guess we'd see how that turned out.

It occurred to me that in my haste to leave, I'd neglected to grab food for the trail. I had a little venison jerky in my saddlebag but not nearly enough for a week's ride across some rough landscape. I did have my guns and plenty of ammunition, but lead isn't too tasty. I'd have to bag me some grub sooner than later.

It was long about midnight with a full moon overhead, when I had to stop. Nature called, and Tornado needed a break. I hadn't been out of my saddle since the stableboy helped me mount back in Kerrville. Ever-so-carefully, I slid my aching body to the ground, leaning against Tornado for a moment to steady myself. I assured myself that the ride home could only get better as I healed. I let Tornado feast on nearby grasses, as I went off to take care of business. I reckoned that by now, and given my decidedly slow pace, Jones was at least a couple of hours ahead of me.

I had just finished relieving myself, when I heard a rattling. To my left, moonbeams reflected from the scaly hide of a coiled rattlesnake, not four feet from where I stood. He was a big one, too! I slowly lifted my Smith &

Wesson from its holster and swept it real easy-like across the front of my body. I could barely see to aim. I pulled the trigger. Explosion...gunsmoke...and the rattlesnake's head disappeared. Lucky shot. Dinner.

My body fought me, but I built a small fire and cooked up that rattler. Some folks find the very idea of eating rattlesnake unappealing, but I've found it a delicacy. It's far more tender than chicken.

My appetite sated, I led Tornado over to a rock and used it as a sort of stepstool to mount up. I felt a twinge as I sat my saddle, but it wasn't quite so bad as back in Kerrville. As I resumed my travels, I wondered whether Jones was close enough to have heard my gunshot shatter the still night air. That led me to speculate as to whether the fugitive heard the shot. I shrugged and urged Tornado forward.

Nine more days lay ahead. When you're riding the Texas hills alone, it can tax your faculties just to stay awake. I'd occasionally sing to myself, carry on one-way conversations with Tornado, and catch a couple of winks of sleep. Much as it pained me to dismount and mount, I gave my beloved stallion a rest now and then by walking alongside. The weather was with me, as rain clouds floated away many miles from my path.

We followed the Pinta Trail, skirted wide around San Antonio, and eventually reached Campbellton on the Atascosa River. Thus far, I'd lived from the flora and fauna of the land. I decided to stop in Campbellton and buy some food and a bit more ammunition. While there, I swung by the Atascosa County jail and chatted with Sheriff Avant. I told him about my adventures in Kerrville and how I was trying to catch Garth Jones.

"Garth Jones, you say? Yuh got a big fish in yer sights, Ranger Dunn," he counseled. "Hear tell that one's killed a few, nearly all shot in the back."

"I understand that your Captain Hughes is busy on the Rio Grande keepin' an eye out for rebels disloyal to Porforio Diaz. Nasty business down there." He rolled a smoke and lit up. "I ain't seen yer man Jones, but if yuh be anything like yer old man, you'll be ketchin' him."

I thanked Avant for his time. The visit hadn't amounted to anything, but it was good to stay on the good side of local sheriffs.

I returned to the trail. All the while, I strove to keep an eye out for Garth Jones. A day later, the Nueces River, famed for its pecan trees, came into view.

Despite my moving slower than molasses in a January freeze, by the end of the sixth day, I found myself little more than an hour behind him. It surprised me that he hadn't set an ambush for me. I had picked up his trail twice thanks mostly to his being careless with his camping habits coupled with his apparently not being in a hurry. Had I not been in such sorry shape...I stopped myself. I was letting negative thoughts and excuses sneak into my thinking. My wounds were healing. The swaying of my body for hours on end in the saddle had tended to loosen the muscles up my left side. I'd avoided any infection, likely thanks to my original treatment efforts with wooly lamb's ear leaves and cauterization.

It would surely be tougher to accomplish, but I decided to try to get ahead of the fugitive. My dad had drummed into me that it was always preferable to be the hunter rather than the prey. Of crucial importance was not giving him a chance to harm my family. Jones was now traveling in country I knew like the back of my hand. I reckoned he'd avoid San Patricio, as he'd rightly figure that the word of his presence in the region had been blared far and wide.

I laid low during the day, as my familiarity with the landscape enabled me to move more easily at night. I found a shady spot under a pecan tree and gave Tornado what I figured to be a final rest before the final push for home. It was a fair bet that upon reaching Nuecestown, Jones would take the ferry rather than ford the river. I aimed to get there ahead of him, God willing. I grabbed a piece of grass and tried to enjoy the shade and the sound of the river meandering by.

"Whag! What yuh huntin'?" came a familiar voice.

I sat bolt upright, wincing with the pain of the sudden movement.

"Dang Junior, yer awful touchy," exclaimed Buffalo Watts.

I shook my head. "Good to see you, too. How long you been tracking me?"

Watts gave a broad, nearly toothless smile. He put aside his ancient Sharps carbine. "Huntin' a buck with a huge rack an' come upon yer trail. Can't hardly miss old Tornado." He chuckled and pulled up a hunk of dirt. "Wondered jus' what yuh might be doin' out heah in the wilds of *Tejas?* Kinda missed yuh since that vigilante hunt an' that lamebrained bandito."

I proceeded to tell him about my adventures in Kerrville and how I was now chasing down a fugitive named Garth Jones who was threatening my family.

"See yuh got yerself shot up a bit," he observed dryly. "Cassie'll be none too happy 'bout that."

"Last time I took a bullet, it was sort of friendly fire. This one was not the case. I was damned lucky."

"Woman shot yuh, eh?"

"Figured that," I said with a smile. "And the man I'm hunting killed her. It was a messy case," I said.

"Yuh jus' gonna sit there an' jaw, or make coffee?" chided Watts.

"No coffee." I replied.

"Well shucks, son. Jus' so happens." He pulled a bag of grounds from his bag. "Given yer condition, you up fer some help?"

How could any self-respecting lawman confronted by the best hunter in Texas refuse? "I'm fixing to circle around him and confront him at the Nuecestown ferry."

Watts nodded. "Good choice. Lotsa tall grass and brush. Low-lyin' mesquite and them trusty pecan trees. Plenty of places to lay a trap."

I shared Jones's note with Watts.

"Dang, no wonder yer all-fired hot to nab the sono-fabitch." He ambled down to the river and filled the coffee pot, which he proceeded to set on the little fire I'd built while we were talking. "What's he packin'?"

"Sharps carbine and at least one 38-caliber Colt Army Model 1892. I expect he's got a knife and might be carrying a Derringer or some other pocket gun." A good lawman always gets a handle on the weaponry he might face, and I'd done a fairly good job of it with Garth Jones.

"Whew!" exclaimed Watts. "He be packin' fer sure!" He poured us some coffee. "Habit?"

I took a sip of coffee. "You haven't lost you touch with coffee, Buffalo." I looked out thoughtfully at the river. "As to Jones, he's strictly a bushwhacker far as I've been able to learn. He's never faced anyone mano-a-mano."

"Tells us a lot, don't it?" mused Watts. He brought the coffee cup to his lips. Cup and coffee suddenly disappeared in a shower of shredded metal and hot liquid. Part of one of Watts's fingers went with it. Then, we heard the explosive report.

"Damn!" I exclaimed, as I dove for cover behind a pecan tree.

Watts was right behind me and armed, having grabbed his rifle in spite of his lost digit. "Sonofabitch is a sight more savvy than we figured," lamented Watts. The grimness in his face said volumes. A couple of inches and he'd have been a dead man.

"Catch me if you can!" challenged Jones from afar. He sent a parting shot over my head and then left to the echo of hoofbeats.

I snatched a piece of fringe from Watt's coat and used it as a tiny tourniquet to stem the bleeding from his finger stub.

He nodded his thanks.

"I've got some of that wooly lamb's ear in my saddle-bag. We ought to cauterize it, though."

Watts nodded. "All these years I been keepin' my hair an' my fingers. Damn!"

"At least it wasn't your trigger finger, my friend." It was a lame attempt to find a bright side.

"Thet sonofabitch has me angry," growled Watts. "We'll nail his sorry ass!" Then, he smiled. "Ain't much of a shot is he? Plumb clean missed my head!"

Leave it to my old mountain man friend to find humor in a near-death experience. "I'd say we gotta be moving if we hope to turn the tables on him."

"Gotta be right careful. He'll likely be layin' fer us." It didn't need saying, but Watts said it anyhow.

"Wish we had a posse." That musing left me wondering whether Sheriff McTiernan had taken my warning to heart and assembled any kind of defense. While my dad had drummed into me that often the best defense was a great offense, I recognized that the reverse could be true. While I was of a mind that the sheriff could at best protect Heaven's Gate and Nueces County for that matter, I understood that he couldn't have men waiting around for something that might never happen. The rolling prairies around Nuecestown were vast, and there was no telling from what direction Jones might choose to wreak his evil.

Garth Jones might have thought himself pretty doggone savvy with his surprise ambush. We were downright lucky that his aim wasn't true. What Jones didn't reckon on was that he was dealing with one of the best, if not the best woodsman in these parts, coupled with my twenty-plus years of living here. We tracked a route along the north bank of the Nueces River, zig-zagging and doubling back from time to time to avoid giving Jones any kind of easy target. We mostly walked our cayuses to offer lower-profile targets.

A couple of times, Tornado's ears pricked up, but his concern turned out to be coyotes and a couple of rattlesnakes.

"He's going to know that we'll be laying for him at the ferry, Buffalo." I said. I'd been pondering alternatives for setting a trap.

"Don't see him usin' the ferry," noted Watts. "It'd make him a sittin' duck." He scratched his whiskers and winced as he realized he'd used the hand with his recently amputated finger. "A bettin' man would figger him to cross farther downriver. Mebbe Nueces Bay, though I be doubtin' he knows 'bout the shell road."

I'd nearly forgotten what was called the shell road across Nueces Bay. It lay just beneath the water's surface and was composed of seashells. The Indians and a few trail-wise folks used it as a secret shortcut rather than go around the bay.

"I don't figure him to head that far past Nuecestown."

That having been said, I envisioned Jones on the ferry in the middle of the Nueces River. I grinned. Not likely he'd use the ferry. We'd come upon no sign of him crossing the river before reaching the ferry, so we could only make an educated guess as to what he'd choose to do. We found a spot where Jones had cold-camped, then continued eastward. He was now making no attempt to cover his tracks, and that concerned us. At some point, he'd head south to reach Heaven's Gate Ranch and he didn't appear concerned that we knew it.

We were a half-dozen miles west of the Nuecestown ferry, when Watts pointed to a couple of buzzards floating overhead as they often did when awaiting the death of their future meal. We mounted up and urged our mounts forward, keeping wary eyes on our surroundings. For all we knew, Jones might have killed something to lure us into a trap. He'd be guessing right that we'd investigate. I recalled that there was a low bluff around the next bend in the trail. It'd be a perfect ambush spot. Watts and I split up so as to approach it from above and below.

Jones was nowhere to be seen, but a terrible stench filled the air. A man was lying against a pecan tree trunk and bleeding profusely from a slashed throat. His eyes already had the glassy look of death. The buzzards circled lower despite our presence.

I knelt beside the poor fellow. Unable to speak, he gave me a final helpless look and took his final breath. I searched the man's pockets and found a small collection of personal items. His name was Slade Cook. He'd apparently been a ranch hand who was unlucky enough to have crossed paths with Garth Jones. I found a spot near the bluff that was tramped down. Jones had undoubtedly been there awaiting his chance to bushwhack us when this cowboy happened by. Our fugitive didn't want to make any noise, so he had jumped the poor man. I glanced up at the buzzards then over at Watts.

"No time," said Watts with a rueful headshake. "Yer man be close now." The varmints would handle the victim's remains.

I felt pangs of guilt, as we cautiously left the scene.

We decided to turn south. I was determined to put myself between Jones and my family. Given that it was late summer, the Nueces River was running a tad shallow. I was concerned about exposing ourselves, as there was no telling where Jones might be lurking. We decided to dismount and wade across, staying close to our horses and effectively using them as shields. I unfastened my gunbelt and hung it on the saddle horn but in easy reach if my Smith & Wesson was needed. The waters barely reached our stirrups, so it would be a fairly-easy crossing. Importantly, we'd cross one at a time. I went first, while Watts provided any necessary cover from the north bank. Once I reached the south bank, I retrieved my Winchester and provided cover for Watts as he crossed.

We dared breathe sighs of relief upon completing the crossing unscathed.

Rolling over in my mind had been possible routes Jones might take to Heaven's Gate Ranch. Rather than guess at a place to intercept him, I decided it'd be best to head to the ranch. I reckoned that Cassie had already been alerted to the danger. If McTiernan was doing his job, there might even be a deputy or two standing guard.

I was beginning to think that we might have managed to turn the tables on Jones. If he was still intent on using my wife as bait to lure me in, we just might have stalled that plan.

Watts and I rode into Nuecestown. The place was pretty much dead or dying, as the railroad had passed it by a couple of years back. By contrast, Alice—the town named for rancher Richard King's daughter—was booming thanks to those steel rails running through it. The buildings were the same, just gradually falling into disrepair. I thought back to the stories my dad told of the shootings the little ferry town had witnessed. My reminiscing was rudely interrupted by Watts pointing to tracks in the soft earth.

"Those be from thet Jones fella's cayuse," he noted. "Damn fool been here ahead of us."

"How the hell?" I uttered with a tinge of angry frustration.

"He be a slick one, Junior," observed Watts.

"More like slimy. He just oozed on past us," I lamented. "We'd better hustle to Heaven's Gate." As I said the words, I realized that "hustle" was ill-chosen. There were far too many places to set an ambush between Nuecestown and Heaven's Gate.

"You know the secret trail?" asked Watts.

It took us about an hour to reach the *ruta occulta*. Ironically, we almost missed it.

I'd nearly forgotten about the hidden path. We called it by its Spanish name, *ruta occulta*. It was screened by mesquite and anacua interspersed with tall stands of switchgrass and Indiangrass. An arroyo wound its way within the foliage. The route ended a mere fifty feet from our barn. It was so hidden that there was no way Jones would have discovered it. We'd taken to not using it on hunts, because it wasn't fair to our prey. We could get to within a half dozen feet of a deer.

It took us about an hour to reach the *ruta oculta*. Ironically, we nearly missed it. It wasn't practical to travel on horseback. There was barely enough space to travel afoot and lead our horses. It took another hour and a half to reach the barn. We picketed our horses out of sight at the end of the *ruta oculta* and sat on our haunches to observe the scene.

"You see anything?" I whispered.

Watts placed a finger over his lips. Something had grabbed his attention. A horse whinnied loudly in the corral adjoining the barn.

A black-clad figure carrying a rifle dashed from the corral to the corner of the house. This was bold as hell. Did Jones think we'd lost him?

I saw a sheriff's deputy appear at the opposite corner of the house. He froze at the sight of Jones.

Garth Jones was quick. His Sharps came up. He aimed and put a slug clean through the poor deputy's chest. The explosion in the still midday air could have awakened the dead. Jones dropped to his knees and made a quick scan for more threats. He didn't see us.

I prayed that Cassie wouldn't come out to investigate. In any case, it was time for me to take charge before there was further bloodshed.

Watts had already taken a bead on Jones.

I gently touched his arm, shook my head, and pointed to my Texas Ranger badge. Justice must prevail. I levered a round into my Winchester and aimed at Jones. "Garth Jones! Drop your gun and raise those hands. You're under arrest," I commanded.

Jones stood and looked in the direction of my voice. He smiled and took a gander at the mesquite tree I was kneeling behind. It admittedly wasn't much cover from any bullets. The murderous fugitive slowly and confidently raised his Sharps to take aim. It was as though he dared me to shoot him.

I squeezed the trigger of my trusty Winchester. It didn't let me down. The slug hit the receiver of Jones's carbine and blew off most of his right hand. The rifle and pieces of his hand went flying in a bloody shower.

"Arrrgh!" howled Jones. He turned and headed on a mad dash toward the corral.

Watts got off a shot with his own Sharps and blew Jones' hat from his head along with a few hair fragments. I emerged, levering and firing as fast as I could at Jones.

The sonofabitch made it to his saddle and galloped off as fast as his cayuse's legs could carry him.

As feared, Cassie appeared at the back door. At least, she needn't fear any return fire from the severely wounded fugitive. "Lucas!" she called. "Lucas!"

I stepped from the mesquite, hurried to her side, and swept her into my arms. Jones was gone. It had been far too close. I shielded Cassie's eyes from the dead deputy sheriff. Watts managed to drag the body to an out-of-sight spot near the barn. Poor Sheriff McTiernan would be none too happy, nor any relatives of the lawman.

Cassie pulled back and looked up into my eyes. "What's going on?" It was the natural question to ask.

"Long story, sweetheart."

She absentmindedly fingered the Texas Ranger badge pinned to my chest as though accommodating the life of a lawman's wife.

"A fugitive from the law was fixing to use you to get at me. But in his evil thinking, he first reckoned to cause me the pain of losing you."

"Is he dead?"

Regret surged through me as I shook my head. "He's

sorely wounded and on the run," was the best assurance I could offer. Buffalo Watts's marksmanship and my delivering a hail of bullets had failed to bring Jones down. I reckoned he'd run off and heal up before coming back to get me. Hatred was a hell of a motivator for evil folks. The Texas Ranger in me wondered whether Captain Hughes would let me track Jones down or leave it to someone with no personal grudge.

Watts strolled up with our horses in tow.

Cassie had wrapped her head around the situation. Apparently, Sheriff McTiernan had warned her of the threat, so the only upset for her was the shooting that erupted upon Jones's arrival. Sean was secure inside our house. She looked at Watts and smiled. "You always inclined to bring this sort of excitement to Heaven's Gate, Buffalo? Are you and my sweet husband here adding lawbreakers to your list of big game?"

Watts offered an aw-shucks shuffle.

Cassie took a gander at his damaged hand and pulled back with concern. "You'd better have a doctor take a look at that," she exclaimed.

Watts looked at the bandage I'd placed on the wound. "Ain't got infected none," he observed. "Junior heah makes a mighty fine doc."

I was about to bask in my new fame as a doctor when we turned to the sound of hoofbeats. Sheriff McTiernan was sitting astride a fairly well-lathered horse.

"What's happened? I heard gunplay," he announced breathlessly. By the expressions on our faces, he could see that he'd missed the action.

"Garth Jones shot it out with us, Sheriff. He's sorely wounded but escaped." I took a deep breath. "I'm sorry to say that Jones killed one of your deputies."

McTiernan dismounted. "Where is he?"

"I drug him outta the line of fire, Sheriff," said Watts. "He's lyin' o'er by yonder barn."

The sheriff strode over to the deputy's body.

I could see McTiernan's neck grow red with anger. "Damn murderer. Chuck had a wife and three kids."

A wave of guilt swept through me. If I'd stopped Jones earlier, it never would have come to this. "I...I'm sorry, Sheriff."

McTiernan saw my guilt-ridden demeanor and softened. "Being a lawman isn't easy, Junior. It's not your fault, son." He tried to ease my burden.

My mind harkened back to the cowboy back along the Nueces River that we'd failed to bury. "We'll hitch up the wagon and carry his remains wherever you'd like, Sheriff. Garth Jones also murdered a cowpoke the other day up west of here. I've got his personal effects in my saddlebag."

McTiernan's eyes widened. "The man was the Grim Reaper. What a sonof..." He caught himself. "Sorry, ma'am," he said with a nod to Cassie.

She smiled. "Call it as you see it, Sheriff." Her eyes swept the faces of the three of us standing there, feeling a mix of emotions ranging from anger to guilt to sorrow. "Come on in, and I'll brew y'all some coffee." She squeezed my hand as I led the way into our kitchen.

★ ★

Garth Jones slipped from the saddle of his heavily breathing, well-lathered horse. He released reins slick with his blood. Looking at the mangled mess that was his right hand, he cursed the Texas Ranger. He'd underestimated his foe and paid a dear price. He tightened the tourniquet around his wrist. The pain was excruciating. The fugitive looked back from whence he'd come. "I won't forget you, Lucas Dunn," he hissed.

Jones took a swig of water and remounted. He needed a doctor, but had to escape these parts before a posse could be mustered. There'd be plenty of time for revenge.

We sat there for the next hour recounting the events of the past few days. Of course, I was able to fill in what transpired up in Kerrville.

"What's next, Junior?" asked Watts, as we sat around the kitchen table sipping coffee and enjoying fresh-baked bear sign.

"I reckon we'll see Jones again, but not until after his hand heals. Buffalo's slug might have taken a piece of the man's scalp, though it likely knocked no sense into the man. I expect I'll send a report to Captain Hughes. Sheriff McTiernan might be so kind as to issue a poster on Jones, maybe up any reward."

"I'll look into that, Junior."

Cassie had been sitting there taking in the conversation. "Well, gentlemen, I've got to get dinner started. Are you staying? Buffalo? Sheriff?"

"Thanks kindly, but I'd better be on my way, Mrs. Dunn. I'll borrow that wagon, if y'all don't mind." McTiernan arose and made his farewells.

Buffalo Watts glanced from Cassie to me and back. "I really outta be moseyin', Cassie. Thanks fer the offer, but home cookin' ain't my style." He quaffed the rest of his coffee, stood, and turned to me. "Yer a top-notch Texas Ranger, Junior. Twas a treat to work with yuh agin'." With that, he headed for the door.

Cassie and I were left alone.

I stood and took her in my arms.

As we embraced, her hands felt bulges of the dressings I had on my wounds. "Lucas! You've been wounded!"

I nodded.

"Well, let me see to those," she insisted and began stripping off my shirt.

I reckoned I was going to appreciate being nursed.

Garth Jones remained a problem to be dealt with. He would be out there somewhere, likely delivering some sort of evil as his wounds healed. McTiernan was good to his word, as a wanted poster was sent out offering a respectable reward for Jones—dead or alive.

I sent a report to Captain Hughes and expected him to call me south to join Texas Ranger Company D on the Rio Grande. I received a welcome response, as he sent a commendation letter acknowledging my success in resolving the murders in Kerrville. My reward was a bonus and a month off for my wounds to fully heal. As to Garth Jones, Hughes's response was guarded. He didn't put me in charge of pursuing the fugitive, but didn't say not to.

For the next couple of weeks, I lazed about Heaven's Gate, spending time with Cassie and our families. I caught up with some cousins, including former Texas Ranger and now rancher Red John Dunn and his Texas Ranger brother Matthew. In the true spirit of Irish blarney, we enjoyed telling tales of our adventures delivering justice as Texas Rangers.

I even rode with Cassie to visit my cousin Nick Dunn. For the princely sum of twelve dollars, Nick had purchased a prize longhorn from Jim Dobie. Champion was his name, and he sported a championship horn spread of better than nine feet. He was an impressive beast yet docile and sweet as can be.

It was a pleasure to relax and especially wonderful to savor the charms of my wonderful wife. We tried to be respectful of my bullet wounds, but that didn't stop us from enjoying the pleasures of the flesh. Dang, but I married an incredibly sexy woman!

All was going decidedly well until Johnnie Crockett arrived with a note he'd been directed to personally deliver. It was about when my recovery time was drawing to a close. I thanked Crockett, stood on the gallery, and tore open the envelope. "Damn!" I blurted under my breath.

Cassie was sitting on a nearby bench and couldn't miss my exclamation. "What is it, Lucas?"

I strode uneasily over to the bench and handed her the note. It was in what looked to be Garth Jones scrawl, though he'd likely written it with his left hand. She read it aloud, "Watch your back Ranger."

The note was a clear threat. Jones wasn't done with me.

"What's this mean?" asked Cassie, as she reread the unsigned note.

I sighed. "It's from Garth Jones." I needn't have said more.

EPILOGUE

THE NUECES STRIP of 1896 was still mostly a vast prairie of tall grasses and loamy sands stretching as far as the eye could see and beyond. Grasses tended to grow high enough to reach a horse's withers, though stands of live oak, mesquite, and prickly pear cactus brought to the prairie from the south mostly by seed-carrying birds and by cattle droppings had already begun to proliferate. Winds blowing through the wiregrass created their own special music. Brush proliferated, often creating nearly impenetrable barriers owing to the density and occasional thorniness. The Nueces Strip, called "Wild Horse Desert" by some, reached south from the lazily flowing Nueces River all the way to the meandering Rio Grande along Texas' southern border. Its eastern extremity enjoyed the sea breezes wafting in off the Gulf of Mexico from Corpus Christi all the way to Brownsville. Nestled in hills at its northern extreme was the little town of Uvalde, while the semi-arid rolling terrain of Laredo was generally regarded as its far western reach. Rough but serviceable roads were being carved out of the Strip and mostly paralleled the railroads. A form of creative destruction was in full flower. Kerrville is generally regarded as the capital of the Hill Country and lay a day's horseback ride north of Uvalde through some of the prettiest vistas on earth.

Despite its uninviting environment, central Texas drew all sorts of opportunists like moths to a light bulb. Texas remained a prime destination for second chancers, folks who'd met with rough times and looked to restart their lives. Towns, farms, and ranches sprung up at record pace. They were pressed to conquer a challenging terrain. Mottes or small clusters of live oak or mesquite offered occasional shade relief on the sunbaked prairies. The often-dry creek beds and arroyos eventually filled with rain water and emptied into Nueces Bay and...farther to the east...Corpus Christi Bay. Flash flooding was an ongoing fear. Summers? Well, they tended to be hot and humid. Weather was pretty much whatever you wanted, if you waited long enough.

The abundant animal life on the Nueces Strip featured deer, javelina, fox, coyote, lynx, black bear, and mountain lion. Armadillos and prairie dogs competed for prairie real estate. At one point, horses were more numerous on the Strip than any animal, including humans. Occasionally, spotted ocelots and even wolves could be sighted by the practiced eye. Owls, hawks, eagles, buzzards...they abounded. Come spring, wildflowers swept across much of the landscape painted like a huge rainbow, with scarlet sage, hibiscus, daisies, poppies, lilies, and the ubiquitous bluebonnets. Groves of cypress, juniper, and palmetto could be found. Pecan trees drew their sustenance from rich soil along the Nueces River. The very name *nueces* was Spanish for nuts. Cactus, along with yucca and agave, abounded. The Nueces Strip surely served as God's canvas.

If you were on foot, it was advisable to keep an eye and ear peeled for rattlesnakes. They tended to blend in fairly well with their surroundings, so their rattle was often folks' first and only warning of an impending attack. The rattlesnake spawned many a "Texas-ism" like "he's so bad he has rattlesnake fangs and twice the venom" or "he's so tough, he cuddles with rattlesnakes."

Much of Texas history centers around the Nueces Strip. No discussion of it can ever be complete without mentioning that much of the most significant fighting of the Texas War for Independence was fought on and just north of the Nueces Strip back in 1835 and 1836. It was also scene to the first skirmishes of the Mexican-American War of 1846. The Strip was officially ceded to the United States by the Treaty of Guadalupe Hidalgo in 1848, though Texas had already laid claim.

The plentiful and accessible longhorn were for years the "low-hanging-fruit" of the Nueces Strip economy. They were a hardy breed that could withstand the South Texas heat, fend off disease-carrying pests, and carry just enough meat on their bones to make them reasonably profitable to raise. Originally brought from the Iberian Peninsula by early Spanish priests, the longhorns eventually escaped the mostly failing missionaries, proliferated, and roamed wild and free across the prairies. Millions of the beasts soon covered Texas and especially the excellent grazing lands of the Nueces Strip. They competed with those wild mustangs that had also been introduced by the Spaniards. Ranchers were increasingly importing and breeding meatier, shorter-horned breeds like Brahmans, Angus, Herefords, and even Richard King's Santa Gertrudis. Of course, there had been the indigenous buffalo, millions of the beasts. They'd been a staple of the indigenous peoples' way of life until their hides were taken in wholesale slaughters to enrich eastern merchants and scions of fashion. The Texas prairies nevertheless provided plenty of feed for all.

The factor that would ultimately win the West was the family; the larger the better as children grew up in the face of all manner of lurking dangers. Families established the ranches and farms popping up not only throughout the eastern portions of the Nueces Strip but across Texas as a whole. People sought fresh opportunity. The territory east of the 98th meridian, sliced through the very heart of Texas that was fast becoming an economic juggernaut, and the Strip was no exception. Its economy was based on growing cotton and raising cattle and horses. Cotton was bundled and hauled to port for transport to markets in Louisiana and points east while cattle were driven mostly to Texas slaughterhouses. Indians were pushed ever westward, as tribes were overcome by a cocktail of socioeconomic forces, violent conflict, and disease.

While the frontier grew ever westward, there was ongoing worry about the threats posed by Comanche, Kiowa, and Lipan Apache, as well as the rogue marauding bandits from south of the Rio Grande and lawbreaking opportunists from the east. This all served to keep early Texans on this wild and often lawless frontier ever vigilant. It was easy to make the case for calling up companies of Texas Rangers to patrol the Nueces Strip, as they took it upon themselves to go where the military found it politically undesirable. On the other hand, the legislators in the state capital in Austin often were unable to pull together the financial means to fund the necessary companies of Rangers. They had to rely on the US Army, which could be chancy at best, as it was subject to the politics of whomever was in power and the perceiving of real or imagined threats.

Thus, the setting for these later Tumbleweed Sagas is hardly any less challenging than mere decades before. Yet civilization marches inexorably onward, taming the remaining frontier.

A LOOK AT
TUMBLEWEED TUMBLINGS: WESTERN TALES & VERSES

Justice rides hard. Legends ride harder.

Tumbleweed Tumblings is a gripping collection of Western short stories and frontier poetry from Mark Greathouse, author of the *Tumbleweed Sagas*. Step into the untamed world of the American West, where every man has a past, every trail has a price, and honor is earned in blood.

From the deadly cunning of villain Horatio Thorpe to the quiet wisdom of Comanche chief Three Toes, these stories unearth the hidden lives behind Greathouse's most iconic characters. Ride shotgun with Texas Ranger Luke Dunn as he hunts justice across a land where danger waits behind every mesquite tree.

Blending pulse-pounding Western action, vivid historical detail, and the haunting rhythm of frontier verse, this anthology paints a bold portrait of a time when men were made—or broken—by the choices they faced at the end of a six-shooter.

Whether you're a loyal reader of the Tumbleweed Sagas or discovering the series for the first time, *Tumbleweed Tumblings* delivers fast-paced storytelling, unforgettable heroes, and a raw, authentic look at life on the edge of civilization.

AVAILABLE SEPTEMBER 2025

ACKNOWLEDGMENTS

Authoring books simply doesn't happen in a vacuum. The author provides the creative talent and crafts the stories, but there's so much more that demands acknowledgment. There's lots of folks and places that contribute to my authoring endeavors. So, it is with *Guns on the Guadalupe: Justice on the River*. It takes place in 1896. The epic exploits of the legendary Texas Ranger Captain Luke Dunn were at the core of the Sagas, but this novel stands apart. At its core, it is also about the taming of the Nueces Strip. Its protagonist symbolizes the lawman image, the pursuer of law and order in the person of a hero, protector, knight-errant sort of character. But there's much more to him. He embodies a family legacy of grit, tenacity, rugged individualism, and bravery nuanced with a masculine vulnerability and a search for redeeming values. He epitomizes the freedom of America's western frontier and represents a final bastion of honor in America. Hopefully, readers will find *Guns on the Guadalupe: Justice on the River* an adventure worthy of their time and emotional involvement.

I've been blessed with many friends and family who have supported my writings. My wife Carolyn's reviews and encouragement were a huge help, along with very important tech support from our sons Mike and Matt. Other supporters have included Cara Miller, Jim May, Ernie Angell, Chris Haug, and my dear cousins Johnny Dunn, Jim & Cindy Holmgreen, Francette Meaney, and Eddie and

Nancy Thornton. Many more friends have contributed support at some level to the creation and publication of *Guns on the Guadalupe: Justice on the River*, be it encouragement or advice.

Naturally, I am major grateful to the great folks at Wolfpack Publishing. The team they bring to publishing is first-rate from editing to typeset to cover design and the myriad tasks that lead to successful book sales.

It's only right to acknowledge my ancestors who were actual settlers of the south Texas frontier. In addition to inspiring me, they provided a quite helpful true-to-life framework as to the life and times on the Texas Nueces Strip. It was appropriate to weave them into the tapestry of my western novels. Matthew Dunn (1809-1863) immigrated to Corpus Christi from County Kildare in 1845, established a homestead on Upriver Road in Nuecestown, and served as a sutler to General Zachary Taylor's Army in the Mexican-American War. Peter Dunn (1807-1890) immigrated from Ireland in 1850 and established a blacksmith shop in Corpus Christi, John Dunn (1803-1889) ranched and grew thousands of acres of cotton, Lawrence Dunn (1837-1864) fought and died with Captain Ware's Confederate cavalry, and my great great grandfather Nicholas Dunn (1835-1912) was a rancher, drover, livestock speculator, marksman, and Comanche fighter of some repute. My cousin John Beamond "Red John" Dunn (1851-1940) served as a Texas Ranger in the 1870s under Captain Bland Chamberlain (Company H), subsequently joined a vigilance committee, became a farmer and merchant, and curated a museum of military weapons displayed to this day in the Corpus Christi Museum of Science & History. Red John Dunn's brother, Matthew Dunn, also served as a Texas Ranger, and another cousin, Rut Evans, served as a Texas Ranger in the 1890s (Company E, Frontier Battalion, Alice, TX). My cousin

Patrick Dunn was quite successful at raising longhorns on North Padre Island east of Corpus Christi from 1883 to 1937. John Hillard Dunn (1883-1958), whose personal narrative about his family and his own adventures drove my pursuit of my Texas family, inspired my own writings, and led me to write his yet-to-be-published biography *Tough Hombre—Recollections of a True Texan*. Finally, my grandfather, Horace Charles Greathouse, served as a Texas Ranger in 1920 (Company C, Austin, TX). Such real-life characters, coupled with actual events, have served to reinforce the historical settings for my writings.

Most of my authoring has occurred in my office as decorated to channel my inner Texan, but my creative juices have often been inspired and imagination stoked in cafés and coffee houses across America. My favorites were Hester's Café & Coffee Bar in Corpus Christi, TX; Nueces Café in Robstown, TX; Java Ranch Espresso Bar & Café in Fredericksburg, TX; PAX Coffee & Goods in Kerrville, TX; Ragged Edge Coffee House and Bantam Coffee Roasters in Gettysburg, PA; 1889 Coffee House in Helena, MT; Dunn Brothers Coffee in Rapid City, SD; Postmasters Coffee & Bakery and Brio Coffeehouse in Waynesboro, PA; Birdie's Café and American Ice Co Café in Westminster, MD; and Baltimore Coffee & Tea Co., Frederick Coffee Company & Café, Deja Brew Coffee in New Oxford, PA and Deja Brew at Miney Branch in Carroll Valley, PA; and Dublin Roasters in Frederick, MD. And yes, I've quaffed my share of coffee at Dunkin' Donuts and Starbucks around America. The décors and easy-listening music in these fine establishments, combined with friendly clientele and savory cups of coffee, tended to set me in the right creative frame of mind.

Last but not least, I'm especially thankful for the many folks who have read and enjoyed my books.

I do believe it is important to acknowledge how the old

west represents the brave pioneering spirit of settlers that met the challenges and transcended mere survival to enable America to achieve exceptional growth. The settling of the American west is replete with tales of leveraging freedom for individual achievement. I hope you will agree that reliving our past—even through history-based fiction—often has the effect of pointing the way to an ever-brighter future. Might we be up to it? I hope that the inspiration I have drawn from my having walked the very earth my characters have trodden, coupled with my extensive historical research, will enable readers to fully experience the grit, adventure, and passion of my characters while sensing aromas of gunsmoke, trail dust, leather, sweat, and bluebonnets.

Thanks kindly to all of you.

ABOUT THE AUTHOR

 Multiple-award-winning author Mark Greathouse is a fifth-generation Texan devoted to history and writing western genre fiction. He has published fourteen western novels, an anthology, and a biography, as well as published western history articles in various magazines and newspapers. He received a 2025 Western Writers of America Spur Finalist Award for Short Fiction with "Prairie Dog" published in a local anthology. *Guns on the Guadalupe: Justice on the River*, published by Wolfpack Publishing, continues Greathouse's passion for weaving fiction in a historical setting. He crafts an engaging adventure, featuring an ensemble of captivating characters woven into compellingly complex subplots. Importantly, he has stayed true to the western story being America's morality story, as good triumphs over evil. Whether expressed in his epic western genre novels or adventure-laced biographies, he couples a soul-penetrating creative spirit with extensive historical research that attracts a broad spectrum of readers. Greathouse is a member of Western Writers of America and several poetry societies. He holds BA and MBA degrees. Greathouse lives in Southern Pennsylvania but travels west regularly to walk in the footsteps of his characters.